LOVE ON STRIKE

Lillie tried to think of something to say. She began, "I want you to know how much I appreciate all the hard work you've been doing for the fund-raiser . . ."

"For the homeless kids," Jay corrected.

"Whatever. Anyway, I appreciate it."

He gave her a half-smile. "Thanks."

Lillie said impulsively, "Let me buy you a malt at Papa's."

"Papa's?" Jay grimaced. "It's so . . ."

"High school?" she finished for him. "Afraid it might ruin your image? Tell you what—you can call it research for your next cartoon in the *Newton News*." Lillie couldn't believe she was being so bold. Maybe he didn't want to spend any more time with her than he had to. "If you have other plans . . ."

"I don't," Jay said quickly. "Let's go." He touched her elbow, making her skin tingle. "I think you should go first." He straightened the collar of his leather jacket as he admitted, "I've never been to Papa's before."

Lillie wanted to laugh, but she thought better of it. Instead, she said solemnly, "You'll *love* the malts!"

Don't miss the exciting three-book mini-series
PRIVATE EYES, inspired by Sweet Dreams #113.
Look for #1 PARTNERS IN CRIME
         #2 TUG OF HEARTS
         #3 ON DANGEROUS GROUND

Bantam Sweet Dreams Romances
Ask your bookseller for the books you have missed

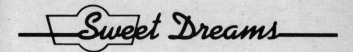

LOVE ON STRIKE

Janice Boies

BANTAM BOOKS
NEW YORK • TORONTO • LONDON • SYDNEY • AUCKLAND

RL 6, age 11 and up

LOVE ON STRIKE
A Bantam Book / October 1990

To Colorado Romance Writers for their friendship and support during my time in Denver

Chapter One

"A *jump-a-thon*?" Frank Lewis laughed from the back of the room where the student council was meeting. "Don't get me wrong. The idea of raising money for the kids at the homeless shelter is great. But why do we have to jump rope to do it?"

Standing at the front of the room, Lillie Evans presented her case. "We agreed it would be best if some of the children could participate—"

"Yeah, I know," Frank interrupted. "The kids are supposed to inspire the students. But do we have to *jump rope*?"

Bob Wilson, the council president, looked at Frank. "Any better ideas? A bake sale? A giant garage sale?"

"A picnic. I bet the kids would love a day in the country," Frank answered.

Lillie's best friend, Karin, nodded with enthusiasm. "We could have three-legged races, and a softball game, and—"

Lillie shook her head impatiently, her shoulder-length dark blond hair falling toward her face. The activity committee had already made their plans. Now everybody wanted to make changes, including Karin.

"Your ideas sound like fun, Karin. But we have only a week to arrange this thing. We don't have time to deal with the park district or worry about rain on a picnic day."

"Then have an open gym night," Frank suggested.

Lillie imagined small homeless children waiting for the big high school boys to share the basketball court. The event needed to focus on the children. But the trick was convincing the Newton High students to be part of a kids' activity.

She gazed at her fellow student council members. "Think about the children. *Small* children. They're looking forward to being part of this. So we need to choose something they can do and something they *like* doing. The way I see it, we can play trucks with them, color with them, or jump rope with them."

"I give up. I'll jump till my feet hurt." Frank raised his hands in surrender, and the two faculty advisors laughed. Then he added, "But Lillie, I don't think even *you* can convince more than ten Newton kids to spend a night jumping rope."

"But it's such a good cause," Lillie told him. She had put together and promoted enough student council activities to know the jump-a-thon wouldn't be easy. But how could anyone ignore the homeless children in Middleton, Minnesota?

Their town was a modest suburb of Minneapolis, and the city had decided to sponsor day care for the children so their parents could look for work. Any money the Newton High students raised would be a great help.

Bob cleared his throat. "It seems the discussion is finished. All those in favor of holding a jump-a-thon to raise money for the new day-care project for the homeless in Middleton . . ."

Lillie tucked her hair behind one ear and raised her hand. To her relief, it looked like everyone else was agreeing with the plan.

"Anyone opposed?" Bob checked the room and saw no hands in the air. "The motion passes. Lillie, how are you going to promote this fund-raiser?"

Lillie twisted the chain of her favorite locket between her fingers. She was determined to convince them the plan would work. "First, we'll get everyone involved with pledging . . . you know, the jumpers will pick up forms and get people to promise to pay for however long they can jump. And then we have to make the jump-a-thon night sound exciting enough to convince everyone to show up."

"How can you do that?" Frank asked skeptically.

"The pledging shouldn't be hard. Everyone loves a reason to talk to people." Lillie knew some girls who actually looked forward to collecting signatures for pledge sheets and petition forms.

She wished Frank would stop asking questions. She realized they were going to face problems, but if Frank would give her half a chance, she'd try to explain her ideas.

"Don't you want the jump-a-thon to sound like *the place* to be next Thursday night?" Bob asked.

"Sure. We can have tapes, or maybe get a radio station to play special music for us . . . and what about pizza for everyone who stays till the end?"

"We don't want to eat up all the profits." Bob grinned.

4

"Of course not," Lillie said. "I'll talk someone into donating the pizzas."

"Super."

"But how are we going to let everyone know in time? It's a week from tomorrow," Karin pointed out.

Bob nodded. "You're right. We don't have much time. We need a dynamite promotional campaign."

Lillie smiled. Bob loved to make their student council meetings sound like big business deals.

"I think you'll need a miracle," Frank muttered.

"Well, we do need something new and different. . . ." Karin tapped her pencil on her notepad as she thought.

"What's wrong with posters?" Lillie asked. "The poster campaign could show everyone how much fun they could have while they're helping these kids."

Karin shrugged. "Posters are fine, but we need something catchier than the usual slogans —something to make people really sit up and take notice."

"Any bright ideas?" Lillie couldn't help feeling a little irritated. It was beginning to sound as if Frank was right. They seemed to be expecting a miracle.

5

"There's always Jay Carson," Frank suggested.

"Perfect!" Bob declared. "Everybody will notice Jay's posters, as long as he doesn't get carried away with his doom-and-gloom stuff."

"Jay Carson?" Lillie repeated.

From her chair at the side of the room, Ms. Henderson, one of the advisors, added, "That's a wonderful idea. Jay could make this promotion different from all the others."

Usually Lillie respected Ms. Henderson's opinion but she didn't agree with the teacher now. Jay Carson was the senior who did cartoons for the school paper, the *Newton News*. His cartoons weren't the kind that made you laugh out loud. They made you think. Sometimes he made fun of the kids at Newton who worried about their clothes but never gave a thought to the thinning of the ozone layer. Other times he didn't include any high school kids and drew cartoons about political issues.

"I think Jay could add a new dimension to this project," Vice Principal McFadden, the other faculty advisor, agreed.

Lillie glanced at Bob. "Are you serious about this? You really want me to ask Jay to do some posters?"

Bob shrugged. "If we care about those kids, we'll find a way to get Jay on our side."

*   *   *

Lillie waited until after school to look for
Jay. Since the student council meeting had
been held before first period, she'd had plenty
of time to worry, and plenty to worry about.

During the last student council elections,
one of Jay's cartoons had made Bob look like
a fool. Jay had drawn a caricature of Bob as a
frog, a frog that thought he could be a prince
if he only got enough votes. But in Jay's cartoon strip, the frog won the election and re-
mained a frog wearing a huge crown that fell
over his eyes. He obviously thought Bob didn't
deserve the job. Lillie dreaded the thought
that he might draw a nasty caricature of her.

Although Jay came to school every day, he
didn't really seem to fit in. He didn't come to
pep rallies or wear something blue on School
Colors Day—he *always* wore his old leather
jacket, and a gold stud in one ear. He was
very tall, and his dark hair was much longer
than the other boys', curling over his jacket
collar. In Lillie's opinion, Jay Carson seemed
to think he was better than everyone else,
and he acted as though school activities were
too childish for him.

"But that's not what I want him to do," she
told herself as she headed toward his locker.
She wasn't asking him to draw cute posters

7

for the prom or anything like that. How could anyone say no to the children? Lillie took a deep breath. She was proud of her cause. Now all she had to do was convince Jay.

She found him bending over, peering intently into his locker. Lillie coughed, but he didn't pay any attention. She had to say something, but what?

She decided to try the humorous approach. "Is there something alive in there?"

He glanced over his shoulder and Lillie's breath caught in her throat. His dark brown eyes seemed to fasten on hers for a very long time. Then he blinked.

"No—why? Do you think I keep a pet in my locker?" When Lillie said nothing, he straightened up and teased, "Are you from Newton High's Animal Control Squad?"

"No. I'm Lillie Evans . . ." was all she could manage to say. He was much taller than she, and up close he was much better looking than she remembered. His dark hair was wavy and kind of wild, but his eyes were steady and watchful.

He nodded. "I'm Jay Carson."

"I know."

He raised one eyebrow. "Well, Lillie, if you're not looking for hidden animals, how can I help you?"

She took another deep breath and crossed her fingers for luck. "The student council wants to donate some money to the city's program to provide day-care services for the homeless kids in Middleton . . ." She lost track of her thoughts when he started to look interested. His dark eyes were very distracting.

"And you're planning a fund-raiser."

Lillie wasn't sure how to interpret his words. It sounded as if he was making fun of the student council and their monthly fund-raising projects.

"To help the kids?" he asked.

"Yes." Lillie mustered a smile as she got her brain under control. "We want the whole school to be involved. It's a very good cause," she added earnestly.

"It is. Count me in."

Lillie stared at him. Had he actually agreed so easily?

One corner of his mouth turned up in a hint of a smile. "What's the deal?"

"A jump-a-thon," Lillie announced boldly.

"A *what*?" There was a teasing edge to his voice when he asked, "What did you have in mind? Skipping? Hopscotch? Broad jump? High jump?"

Lillie laughed. "Jump rope."

9

Jay whistled and the sound echoed in the empty hall.

"Will you still help?" she asked, hoping he wouldn't think it was so silly that he'd change his mind.

"Sure," he answered. "Why not? What would you like me to do?"

"Posters," Lillie said promptly. "We want you to design posters so eye-catching and so different that everyone will want to participate."

Jay rocked back on his heels and seemed to stare into space. Suddenly he said, "Do you want to focus on the kids and how much we can help them?"

"That might inspire people to grab pledge sheets and get signatures, but we'll need to do something really special to encourage them to actually show up on Jump Night. It's scheduled for next Thursday, so we don't have a whole lot of time. If you could just do some posters that would convince everyone how great it will be . . ."

"Jumping?"

"Yes, jumping." She raised her chin and looked him right in the eye. "Can you do that?"

He rubbed his chin. "It's a challenge. Want to help?"

10

"Excuse me?" It sounded like a line, the kind of thing a guy would say if he liked a girl and was leading up to asking for a date. But Jay Carson couldn't possibly want to go out with her. And if he *did* want to see some girl, Lillie was sure he was the type to just come right out and ask her.

Jay seemed to read her mind. "Hey, this is nothing personal. But you know the kind of work I usually do, and frankly I'm a little skeptical about a jump-a-thon. Maybe you can make sure I don't come up with something too silly or too . . ."

"Cynical?" Lillie suggested.

"I suppose you could put it that way. Those kids deserve the best. So will you help me?"

"Sure," Lillie agreed. "When should we get together?"

"How about tomorrow after school?" he asked. "I need some time to come up with a concept."

"That'll be fine. Should we meet here?"

"If it's easier I can meet you somewhere else. Your locker?" he offered.

"No," Lillie answered quickly. She could just imagine what her friends Karin and Gina would say if Jay Carson came strolling down the hall to pick her up.

"What's the matter? You have a problem?" Jay's dark brown eyes studied her.

Lillie felt her cheeks grow warm and wished she didn't blush so easily. "No problem. I'll meet you here tomorrow afternoon. Same time, same place."

Chapter Two

"Did you have any luck coming up with a concept?" Lillie asked when she met Jay the next afternoon.

He nodded toward the notebook tucked under his right arm. "I have some ideas."

They began to walk down the hall together. Jay walked like someone who was very sure of himself, and Lillie had to struggle to keep up with him.

"Where should we go?" he asked.

"The student council room should be empty." All student council work was done in a room on the second floor, but Lillie couldn't quite imagine Jay Carson sitting behind one of those little tables. "Will that be all right?"

"We can give it a try." He made it sound as if he were doing her a favor.

Jay followed her up the stairs, and Lillie realized he probably didn't have any idea how to find the student council room on his own. "It's halfway down this hall," she told him when they got to the second floor.

When they arrived, Jay paused in the doorway and shook his head. "I'll try to work in here."

He pulled out the chair closest to the door and then sat down, stretching his long legs out in front of him. Lillie thought he looked like a prisoner desperate for freedom.

She sat in the chair next to his and eyed his notebook. "What have you got?"

Jay opened the cover and pulled out several loose sheets, making sure they were in order before he started to explain his plan.

"We need two parts to this campaign, right?"

"Sure," was all Lillie could say.

"In the first part, we need to tell people how much the children need their help and to introduce the jump-a-thon idea, and finally to hint about what a terrific time they'll all have jumping rope next Thursday night." Jay suppressed a smile as he mentioned a roomful of happy rope-jumpers.

"And what about the second part?" Lillie asked.

"We'll drive them into a frenzy, tempting

them with clues about all the dynamite activities you have planned."

Now she knew he was teasing. Lillie frowned. "I thought you were taking this project seriously. A week from today we're going to have dozens of homeless children in the gym, expecting to jump rope with the big guys, no matter how silly you think it sounds. It'll be fun for the kids, and the money we make will really help."

Jay leaned back until the front legs of his chair raised off the ground. He crossed his arms over his chest and turned to look at her. He looked for a long time, studying her hair and face, though his dark eyes didn't give any hint that he was interested. She shifted uncomfortably in her chair. "Do you have some sketches or something to show me?"

His chair legs hit the floor with a thud. "Yeah."

He began to spread out his papers on the table. The sheets were covered with rough sketches that Lillie couldn't see clearly unless she leaned closer to Jay, and she wasn't quite sure she wanted to do that.

"Okay. Here's what I have in mind. We'll put up a series of posters all over the school

15

each day. The students will have to find all of them and put the puzzle together."

"That sounds great!" Lillie was impressed.

Pointing to the sketch at the far end of the table, Jay said, "The first day, Monday, the posters will show kids telling why the day-care service is important to them—their parents can look for jobs, and the kids themselves will get a real lunch. And in the corner of each poster, there'll be a jump rope and a note about pledging or something. . . ." He looked up at Lillie. "Where will they get the pledge sheets?"

"Here in the student council office."

"Right. I'll put the room number on, too." His finger traced over the next row of papers. "Now these are the kind of things we'll put on the posters on Tuesday—more about pledging, something about getting your feet in shape, something else about the children. And the jump rope logo will stay in the corner."

"Sounds neat!" If he could make the campaign work as well as it sounded, it would be worth the nervous attack she'd suffered over meeting him.

He nodded as if he knew his plan was good. Then, running his hand through his long, dark hair, he asked her, "Are you hungry?"

Lillie blinked. "What?" Wasn't he going to explain the rest of his ideas?

"Lillie, I just can't think in here. It's so . . ." He looked around the room as if searching for the right words. "It's so *official*. I don't belong here."

She told herself he was an artist and she should try to understand, even if she really couldn't. "What do you want to do?"

"I'd like to discuss this in a more relaxed place, with some food in front of me."

"Okay." Lillie glanced at her watch. Her parents didn't expect her home for another hour. With an unsure smile, she told him, "I could use a soda."

"All right." He quickly packed up his papers and was out in the hall in seconds, Lillie at his heels.

She expected they'd go to Papa's House across the street from school, since all the kids from Newton hung out there. But Jay marched in the other direction, into the school parking lot toward an old green Volkswagen bug.

"It's probably not what you're used to, but it runs," he told Lillie as he held the door open for her.

She waited until he had gotten in before

17

she answered, "I'm not fussy. I'd love to have a car—any kind of car—of my own."

He raised his eyebrows. "Won't your dad buy you one?"

Lillie laughed. "My dad is a history teacher here at Newton High. We don't have the money for an extra car."

"I see." Jay didn't say anything more as he drove the Volkswagen out of the school parking lot.

Had he really believed she was rich? Lillie was amused by the thought. Then she realized she didn't know where he was taking her. In fact, it occurred to her that she didn't know much about Jay Carson at all. She cleared her throat. "Uh, where are we going?"

He slowed for a stoplight. "The Dive."

"Isn't that over by the university?" When he nodded, she told him, "I've never been there before."

"Don't worry," Jay said as if he sensed her apprehension. "You'll be with me."

It sounded as if he was a regular at The Dive. And Lillie discovered that indeed he was when the cook greeted him from behind the counter and several of the college students knew him by name. He led her to a booth near the back of the café.

"Hey, Sally," he said as a waitress approached. "I'll have a double cheeseburger—rare—a basket of fries, a vanilla malt, and . . ." He gazed across the table at Lillie. "What do you want?"

"Diet orange, please." As soon as the waitress left, she asked, "You can eat all that before dinner?"

"This *is* my dinner," Jay told her.

Lillie stared at him. "Don't you eat with your family?"

He laughed. "I usually do. But my folks' plane won't land until late tonight."

"Were they on vacation?" Lillie asked, picturing the Carsons on some beach in the Caribbean.

"My dad had to go get some award in Detroit," he said casually.

"Award? What does he do?"

"He's a lawyer."

"What kind of awards do lawyers get?" Gina's dad was an attorney, but Lillie had never heard about Mr. Portelli winning anything.

"My dad is C. J. Carson." When Lillie didn't recognize the name, he added, "He's a civil liberties lawyer."

"*That* C. J. Carson?" Lillie was impressed. "We talked about him in social studies last quarter!"

19

"That's my dad."

Lillie could tell Jay was proud of his father. Now she was beginning to understand why Jay Carson was so different from the other kids at Newton. Growing up with a father who was on the national news at least once a month had to be a very different experience from living in a suburb with a high school history teacher.

Jay patted his notebook. "Shall we get back to the jump-a-thon?"

"Sure." Lillie flashed him an encouraging smile and was surprised when he looked embarrassed. Maybe he's not used to girls smiling at him, she thought.

"For Wednesday, each poster should list one good reason to participate."

"Like what?" She couldn't wait to hear some of the benefits of rope jumping.

"It's aerobic exercise." He sounded sarcastic when he added, "Everyone who *is* anyone will be there. And, of course, it's all to help the kids."

"You can add door prizes," Lillie told him. "I've talked some businesses into donating merchandise."

"That's great." He took a closer look at her. "You really *are* taking this seriously, aren't you?"

"Of course I am!" Lillie tried not to show how offended she was. This guy obviously thought she was an airhead. Well, he'd find out that he was wrong before the jump-a-thon poster campaign was over.

He turned the last two sheets toward her. "On Thursday, we bring out the big artillery. By Wednesday, let me know some of the best prizes you've collected." He sighed. "But, to tell you the truth, we're going to need more than that to ensure a good turnout."

"I'm hoping to get a color TV from Ken's Appliances," Lillie said, though she didn't sound very convincing. Since she was talking about near impossibilities, she decided to tell him about her other idea. "I'd love to get a deejay, but it's pretty short notice. . . ."

"Which deejay?" he asked.

"Maybe someone from WXYZ." But they had about as much chance of getting a WXYZ deejay as they did of convincing the President of the United States to jump along with the rest of them.

The waitress set Jay's cheeseburger, fries, and malt in front of him and gave Lillie her soda.

"That shouldn't be a problem," Jay said.

After he had devoured a handful of fries, he went on. "I can get a WXYZ deejay. You want him to set up in the gym and broadcast from there?"

Lillie choked on her drink. He could get a deejay from WXYZ? To broadcast from the *school*? Sure he could—right!

"Please don't tease me," she snapped. "This deal is supposed to happen a week from today. We don't have time for jokes."

"I'm not joking." Jay sipped his malt. "Believe me, I can do it."

Lillie stared at him, wondering about his sense of humor. Teasing one second and serious the next. Jay Carson was a puzzle.

"Don't do that," he told her.

Lillie wasn't sure what she'd been doing, but she would stop whatever it was if there was any chance that this guy could really deliver a live and breathing deejay from WXYZ. "What should I stop?"

"Staring at me with those big blue eyes."

She blinked. "You don't like blue eyes? Or should I just close them?"

"I like your eyes just fine," he confessed, to her amazement. "But when I said I could get you a deejay, they got even bigger and bluer. I can't handle that."

"And I can't believe you *can* convince anyone from WXYZ to broadcast from the Newton gym."

22

"My dad went to college with WXYZ's station director. He's always willing to run public service announcements for my dad's activities. And he's sent deejays to some of Dad's rallies, too."

"Do you think your dad would—?"

"I'll ask him tonight."

"I don't know what to say!" she murmured.

"*Thanks, Jay* would be fine," he said with a sly smile.

Lillie smiled back. "Thanks, Jay. I don't know what I—I mean, *we*—would do without you."

Chapter Three

"**W**here is Johnny taking you tonight?" Karin asked Gina as they and Lillie walked onto the school grounds on Friday morning.

"A movie, I think." Gina flipped her long, dark, waist-length hair over one shoulder.

"I hope he's not into Rambo." Lillie was never quite sure what to expect from football players.

Karin fiddled with her yellow, banana-shaped earrings. "Are you going to wear your new jeans skirt?"

"I wore that on our last date. I thought I'd wear . . ."

As Gina and Karin chattered on, Lillie had the strange sensation that someone was watching her. She looked around and saw Jay leaning against one of the pillars outside

Newton's front door. Somehow he looked out of place—Jay Carson just didn't seem like the type to hang around doing nothing. Maybe he was just enjoying the cool, sunny May morning. Or maybe he was waiting for somebody.

Gina punched her in the arm. "Hey, Evans! I'm *trying* to ask if your mom has anything exciting in her shop that I could wear for my date tonight."

"Uh . . . I don't know." Lillie couldn't stop thinking about Jay. She'd never seen him checking out all the morning arrivals before.

"I can't believe you," Karin said with a sigh. "If my mother made gorgeous stuff the way yours does, I'd know every single item in the store."

Lillie's friends thought it was great that Mrs. Evans designed and sewed clothes for a little shop she ran in town. Lillie liked the clothes, but she'd worn her mom's creations all her life. It was a treat for her to buy an outfit with someone else's name on it.

Just as they were about to pass Jay, he fell into step beside Lillie.

"Hey, Lillie, got a minute?"

Giving her friends a quick smile, she turned to Jay. "Sure." She could barely swallow past the nervous lump in her throat.

Karin and Gina dawdled along behind. Lillie knew they were dying to hear whatever Jay had to say.

"My dad called his friend at WXYZ last night," Jay told her as they walked into the school.

"And what did he say?" Lillie asked breathlessly.

Jay shrugged. "I told you they were good friends. He said Byron Hoddel would be happy to broadcast from the jump-a-thon next Thursday night."

"And I'm going to the moon on my next birthday!" Lillie said with disbelief. Maybe the station director had said Byron Hoddel would be happy to do it, but had anyone asked Byron?

"I'm serious." Jay grabbed the full sleeve of her mauve tunic, one of her mother's designs. When she looked up in surprise, his hand dropped to his side.

Lillie lowered her gaze. "I just can't believe anyone could get WXYZ's prime-time deejay to make a house call."

Jay impatiently ran a hand through his hair. "Well, my dad did. You're supposed to call Byron after school today with all the details." He pulled a folded piece of paper out of his jeans pocket. "Here's his number."

Lillie's fingers tingled as she held the paper. Byron Hoddel's phone number! He was only the most popular deejay in town. "I can't call him," she whispered, panic-stricken.

Jay snorted. "Just when I was starting to think you weren't one of the mush-brains—"

"*Mush-brains!*" Lillie repeated angrily.

"That's what I call the kids around the school who only care about proms and football games and student council foolishness."

Lillie was furious that he thought so little of her friends, the people who worked so hard for their school. After all, it was *his* school, too. "We're *not* mush-brains. We care about a lot of things!"

He followed her to her locker. "But you don't care enough about the jump-a-thon to call."

She whirled around and glared at Jay. She didn't care whether or not her blue eyes bothered him. "So I'm afraid to call him, okay? He's a big, famous person, and I'm just Lillie Evans, a high school junior—a nobody!"

He studied her for a moment. Then he shook his head and said quietly, "No one has to be *just* a high school student. And you're not a nobody. You're Lillie Evans. And she could be very important if she wanted to be."

Lillie was aware that her friends were close by. How was she going to explain what they had no doubt heard? She didn't understand it herself.

She tucked the folded paper in her pocket. Somehow she'd find the nerve to open it and call Byron Hoddel after school ended. She had to. "Thanks for the help. If you take care of the posters, I'll take care of this," she said to Jay.

As soon as Jay was out of sight, Karin and Gina were at her side. "*What* are you taking care of?" Gina wanted to know.

"Really!" Karin added, her banana earrings jingling with excitement. "What did Jay Carson just give you?"

Lillie decided on the spot to keep the whole thing secret. That way, if Byron turned her down when she called him, she wouldn't be publicly embarrassed. And if he agreed to do it, everybody would be impressed when the first posters for Thursday hit the walls.

She said, "You know I'm working with Jay on the jump-a-thon promotion. . . ."

"That's all?" Karin sounded disappointed.

"Forget Jay Carson." Gina sighed. "We just heard an awful rumor."

Before Gina could continue, Karin jumped in. "Everyone's talking about a teachers' strike. What do you know about it, Lillie?"

"Your dad's a teacher. He must have told you something," Gina said in a rush.

Lillie was surprised. "He hasn't mentioned anything." She took a moment to think. "But come to think of it, he and Mom have been talking quietly a lot and Dad's been looking worried lately."

The first bell rang. The girls had five minutes to get to their homerooms. On their way to the center stairs, they bumped into Ms. Henderson.

"Ms. Henderson," Karin cried. "Is there going to be a strike?"

The teacher looked startled for a second. "I didn't know the students had heard about it."

"Then it *is* true!" Lillie said. Why hadn't her father told her?

"There's nothing definite yet." Ms. Henderson shook her head. "But I have to be honest. It's beginning to look like a real possibility."

"What are you smiling about?" Lillie's father asked as he drove into his space in the school parking lot early on Monday morning.

"I was just remembering the look on your face when Jay called me last night to set up our meeting this morning," she said.

Richard Evans shook his head. "I just didn't realize you knew him."

"Don't you like him?" Her father loved teaching so much that Lillie had always assumed he liked all his students.

"He's an interesting boy," he said. "I've never heard you mention him before."

"I'd never met him before he agreed to help with the jump-a-thon."

Getting out of the car and locking his door, Mr. Evans said, "That's strange. A jump-a-thon doesn't seem to be his style."

Lillie wondered what her father meant by that. What exactly *was* Jay's style? She hadn't yet figured it out for herself, and sometimes she thought she never would.

"I'd love to stay and talk, honey, but someone is waiting for you." Mr. Evans pointed toward the student parking lot, where Jay was getting out of his Volkswagen.

"See you tonight, Dad." Lillie waved as her father headed for the school building. Then she went over to meet Jay.

Jay shook his head as she came up close to him. "You even look good this early in the morning." He groaned. "Don't tell me you're a morning person!"

It was obvious to Lillie that Jay was *not* a morning person. His dark eyes were little more than slits, and he looked as if he was still half asleep.

"Why did you want to meet me at seven-fifteen if you hate mornings?" she asked.

"I don't exactly *hate* mornings," he mumbled. "But I was up until two finishing posters."

"Two A.M.?" When Jay Carson got involved, he apparently gave one hundred and fifty percent. "You didn't have to do that—" Lillie began.

Jay covered his mouth and yawned. "Yes, I did. I have to study for a math test tonight, and we need the second set of posters tomorrow morning."

"Thanks," Lillie said. She couldn't think of anyone else at Newton who would work so hard.

"Want to see 'em?" Jay asked, lifting a stack of poster boards out of his car.

"Right here in the parking lot?"

"Why not?" One by one he held the artwork up for her approval.

"It's great!" she said. The first poster showed a cartoon of a child slurping a bowl of soup. The bubble over the child's head said: IF I CAN GO TO DAY CARE, I CAN GET A HOT LUNCH . . . JUST LIKE YOU. ON SECOND THOUGHT, I HOPE MINE WILL BE BETTER! The jump rope logo and student council room number were printed in the lower right-hand corner.

Lillie smiled at Jay's drawing of the Newton commons—the place where everyone met their friends—on the next poster. But instead of high school students in the commons, he'd drawn toddlers and preschoolers. One little guy was saying: WE'RE JUST LIKE YOU. WE WANT TO GO TO DAY CARE AND HANG OUT WITH OUR FRIENDS. DON'T YOU THINK THE GIRL IN THE PINK DIAPERS IS CUTE?

Lillie laughed out loud. The posters would appeal to everyone who hated school lunches and liked spending time with their friends. And once students realized that they had something in common with the homeless children, Lillie was sure that lots of them would hurry to the student council office for pledge forms.

The cartoons and captions on each poster were guaranteed to make everybody smile. Lillie loved the way Jay had drawn the letters above the soup-slurper's head so they looked like noodles.

"It must have taken you all weekend to do these," Lillie said, awed by Jay's artwork. Drawing was not one of her talents.

"Not really. I've sketched out all the posters, but I've only finished the ones for today and tomorrow. Let's go and hang these babies," Jay suggested, tucking the whole stack under his arm. "I know just where to put them."

Lillie followed him around the school with a roll of masking tape, helping him mount the posters. They put the soup poster outside the cafeteria, where everybody waiting in line would see it. The baby poster went in the commons, where it would be seen every time anyone went in or out. The others were distributed in various hallways, usually next to classroom doors.

"One more," he told her when she thought they were done. His long legs took the stairs two at a time as he headed for the second floor. Lillie had to run to catch up with him.

Jay taped the last poster to the door of the student council office. It was a white sign with the red jump rope logo on it. Beneath the picture big letters announced: THIS IS THE PLACE. GET A PLEDGE SHEET. MAKE A PLEDGE!

Sounding almost shy, he asked, "How do you like it?"

Lillie beamed. Jay had made his feelings about student council "mush-brains" quite clear, but he'd remembered the sign for the office. She was pleased.

* * *

After school, Lillie saw Jay standing near her locker with Lucas Harmon. She'd seen them together often around school, Jay with his earring and Lucas with a red bandanna tied around his head. Like Jay, Lucas was not part of any crowd, and everybody thought he was a little strange.

She didn't think either of them noticed her until she heard Lucas shout, "Blonde alert! Blonde alert!"

Lillie winced. Why was Lucas acting like such a jerk?

Jay turned around. He looked happy to see her. Then, seeing her expression, he frowned. "Is something wrong?"

"Uh, no." Lillie's voice sounded gravelly. She cleared her throat and tried again. "I've been hearing lots of good things about the posters."

Lucas started backing away. "Hey, I gotta go, man."

"See you later," Jay told his friend, although he was still watching Lillie.

She felt guilty. "I didn't mean to interrupt anything."

Jay chuckled and turned to pick up his books from the floor where he'd left them. "We were just talking. It wasn't a big deal."

Now that she seemed to have driven Lucas away, Lillie tried to think of something to

35

say. She began, "I want you to know how much I appreciate all the hard work you've been doing for the jump-a-thon—"

"For the homeless kids," he corrected.

"Whatever. Anyway, I appreciate it."

He gave her a half smile. "Thanks."

"Let me buy you a vanilla malt at Papa's," Lillie said impulsively.

"Papa's?" Jay grimaced. "It's so . . ."

"High school?" She finished for him. "Afraid it might ruin your image? Tell you what— you can call it research for your next cartoon in the *Newton News*." Lillie couldn't believe she was being so bold. Maybe he didn't want to spend any more time with her than he had to. "But if you have other plans . . ."

"I don't," he said quickly.

"Don't you have to study for that math test?"

"I'll have time later. Let's go." He touched her on the elbow, making her skin tingle.

Lillie swallowed hard and smiled at him. "What are you waiting for?"

"I think you should go first." He straightened the collar of his leather jacket as he admitted, "I've never been to Papa's before."

Lillie wanted to laugh, but she thought better of it. Instead, she said solemnly, "You'll *love* the malts!"

*   *   *

36

"And have you ever noticed how the science teachers talk a lot about threats to the environment, but their wastebaskets are full of aluminum soda cans that could be recycled?"

Lillie pushed her empty malt glass out of the way and rested her elbows on the table. Jay had been filling her head with fascinating observations about Newton High for the last forty-five minutes. She almost forgot that they had been going to the same school for the last two years. It seemed like Jay was talking about a totally different place.

"Did you know I tried to convince the cooks in the cafeteria to give the leftover food to a shelter, and they said that the government wouldn't let them do it?"

"Why not?"

"Apparently some higher authority is afraid we'll be cheated if the kitchen people are allowed to keep the leftovers instead of throwing them out. I mean, what if the food servers started giving us poor high school students less vegetables and fruit so they'll have plenty left to take home at night? Logical, right?"

Lillie wrinkled her nose. "I don't believe you! That's crazy!"

He shook his head. "No, that's bureaucracy. So perfectly good food gets thrown into the garbage, and homeless people go hungry."

"What are you going to do about it?"

Jay's shoulders slumped. "Nothing—yet. But sometimes I sneak some leftover bread outside and feed it to the birds."

"You'd do anything to break the rules, wouldn't you?"

"Only the ones that violate the basic laws of human decency."

"You really mean it, don't you?" Lillie murmured softly.

Jay sat back in the booth. "You bet I do. Here's a question for you: Which is more important—attending a mandatory pep rally for the basketball team, or leaving school to go to a seminar on ethics in government?"

Lillie's mouth fell open. "You did that?"

"Which would you have chosen?" he asked, his gaze suddenly dark and intense.

Lillie thought about it. True, pep rallies could get boring. But several hours of hearing about political corruption? "I don't know if I would have picked the heavy stuff," she admitted.

Jay shrugged. "It's your world."

Lillie saw his point. "I guess pep rallies and dances, and even jump-a-thons, must seem pretty stupid to you when you think about, uh, the big picture. . . ."

He reached out, and Lillie's hand met his.

Though only their fingertips touched, Lillie felt an electric tingle all the way down to her toes.

"Don't include the jump-a-thon on that list," Jay said seriously. "And I'm not the only one who thinks about the big picture. A lot of people do. And even if some people don't worry what's going on in the world, we're all in it together."

"So you're trying to make it better for all of us."

"Yeah. For me. For you." Jay's gaze strayed to the table where Bob Wilson was sitting with some other student council officers. "And even for the mush-brains."

Lillie wondered when it had happened. She didn't know the exact time or place, but sometime, somehow, she had apparently been dropped from Jay Carson's mush-brain list.

It was a wonderful feeling.

Chapter Four

"Can you *believe* all the people?" Karin had to shout into Lillie's ear on Thursday evening, to be heard over all the voices and Byron Hoddel, who was testing his microphone. Small children were watching the deejay set up his equipment, and some of their parents were talking with Vice Principal McFadden. Strangely, Ms. Henderson was nowhere in sight.

Lillie asked her friend, "Do you think the little kids are having fun?"

"Look at the way that boy in the red shirt is grinning," Karin said, pointing toward the stage. "I didn't know anyone could smile that big!"

"I'm starting to think this thing is really going to work. Half the school seems to be here." Lillie glanced around the gym, delighted by all the teenagers crowding through the doors.

"But one person's missing. Where's your new friend?" Karin fluffed her short, light brown hair, and the bells in her silver earrings chimed when she brushed them with her hand.

"Who? You mean Jay?" Lillie smiled. "Spending two hours jumping rope isn't Jay's kind of thing. He said he might show up later, but his real contribution was the posters."

"And they were great! Everyone was talking about them all week." Karin tossed her jump rope over her shoulder. "But I thought he wanted to raise money for the kids."

"He does. He pledged to pay ten dollars for every fifteen minutes I jump," Lillie said.

"Wow! That's forty bucks an hour!" Karin's brown eyes sparkled. "What's going on with you and Jay Carson, anyway?"

Lillie laughed, flustered. "Nothing. He just wants to help the children."

Gina rushed up to the two girls, wearing her blue and white cheerleader's outfit. "*Love* your jumpsuit," she told Lillie. "Did your mom make it?"

Lillie nodded. Actually it was one of her mother's creations that she really liked. The aqua jumpsuit was comfortable, besides being very chic, and Lillie always preferred comfort over style.

Karin glanced around the room and asked Gina, "Are all the cheerleaders wearing their uniforms?"

Gina explained, "Diana Fulton thought this event was important enough for the squad to send some representatives . . ."

"Oh, right," Karin said with a laugh. "We all know Diana has a huge crush on Byron Hoddel. I bet she figured he'd notice her in her short little blue and white skirt. Did she bring her pompons, too?"

"Don't be so mean!" Gina protested. "I think it's great that the whole school is involved in raising money for such a worthy cause."

"Is Johnny coming tonight?" Karin asked.

Gina grinned. "I kind of made him promise to show up with some of his friends."

"Thank you," Lillie told her sincerely. "No one is going to call this a boring student council activity if the cheerleaders and the football players are here!"

"Don't forget Byron Hoddel," Karin reminded her. "And Lillie actually got to meet him!"

"Someone had to show him around," Lillie said casually. "Besides, he's really very nice, not full of himself, like I expected."

43

Gina sighed. "It's just so amazing! Anyone who isn't here tonight is going to be sorry when they hear about how much fun we had."

"You haven't had any fun yet, ladies," Bob Wilson told them as he made his way through the crowd. "You still have two hours of jumping to do, remember?"

"I swear," Karin said when he was gone, "that guy could take the fun out of *anything*!"

"Karin Donovan!" Lillie pretended to be shocked. "Bob's the president of the student council!"

But Karin, the secretary of the student council, refused to back down. "I don't care what he is. Sometimes he's a real pain."

Gina giggled. "You know what? You're right!"

"Ladies and gentlemen!" Byron Hoddel's amplified voice seemed to bounce off the gym walls. "It's time to synchronize our watches . . . not that you'll be able to see *yours* when you're jumping . . ." He adjusted his watch to match the time on the wall clocks. "Does everyone have their jump ropes?"

"Yeah!" The teenagers and the little children waved their ropes over their heads, trying their best not to hit their neighbors.

"I've got some rules here to read—" The

kids groaned and Byron told them, "Hey, I'm not a teacher. Give me a break."

First he invited the little children to a corner away from the stage, where they could jump in safety when hundreds of ropes started flying through the air. Then he explained that it was okay to rest if anyone got tired. Water was available at the back of the gym, and pizza would be served at the end of the evening. Those interested in jumping alone should do it close to the stage. Groups were to do their jumping at the back of the gym.

Bob Wilson pushed his way to the deejay and handed him a note. Byron smiled when he read it. "Congratulations, Newton High! So many of you showed up that some of you are going to have to do your thing in the halls so you don't knock each other down. We'll leave the gym doors open so you can all still hear my show."

As he talked, people pushed and shoved to get to the places where they could see the deejay, and Lillie followed Karin to a spot right next to a speaker.

"We'll be *deaf* in two hours!" Lillie hollered.

"Did you say *dead*?" Karin yelled back.

Lillie giggled. "No, dummy. *Deaf*!"

"The countdown!" Byron yelled to get ev-

45

eryone's attention. "Twenty seconds to seven o'clock. Fifteen. Ten . . ."

Everyone started getting their ropes into position. Lillie had to take a step sideways to keep from tangling her red rope in Karin's blue one. She was ready for some serious jumping.

The gym seemed to pulse as all the kids chanted, "Five, four, three, two, one!"

Suddenly, ropes were flying everywhere. Byron hit a switch and the music started, while he spoke into the microphone, welcoming the whole city to his live broadcast from the Newton High gym, where the students were raising money for the city's day-care project for homeless families.

For the first time Lillie realized that Byron might really have wanted to be part of the jump-a-thon, rather than just doing it because his boss owed Mr. Carson a favor. Lillie knew how important it was that so many students had turned out to support the project. And the kids from the shelter seemed to be having a good time, too. Jay would say they were all doing something to improve their world.

Suddenly, there was a lump in her throat and then her eyes started to get all watery.

She tripped over her rope, and took a second to wipe away a tear.

"What's wrong? Something in your eye?" Karin shouted as she jumped.

"Yeah!" Lillie yelled back. Karin would think she was crazy to get so sentimental about a bunch of kids jumping rope.

Lillie didn't think about being thirsty until she saw a girl from the soccer team with her own personal water bottle. When she started to imagine using her rope to lasso the bottle, she knew it was time for a break.

She threw her rope over her shoulder and Karin was quick to follow her example. As they threaded their way through the jumping frenzy, Karin gasped melodramatically. "Water . . ."

On their way toward the refreshment table, Lillie saw Gina and Johnny jumping together, sharing one rope. "Hey, look at that."

Karin sighed and lifted her sweaty bangs off her forehead. "How can they do that? I'd have thought the guys would be tripping over their own feet—especially the football players."

"Don't they use jump ropes in their training? It builds their stamina or something."

Karin groaned. "It must. I don't feel this tired even after I do my mom's Jane Fonda

47

tape. And we've only been jumping for about half an hour."

"Speaking of aerobics . . ." Lillie pointed to a girl from her English class. She was wearing a neon yellow leotard and leggings, and she was circled by a group of admiring guys.

"I wish I had a figure like that." Karin tugged on her fleece top. "I have to cover myself with a sweatsuit when I exercise in public. No wonder I'm so hot."

"I know what you mean." Lillie had no idea how she would look in Lycra, because she had never been brave enough to try it.

They drank some water and then Karin playfully slapped Lillie's back with her rope. "Get back to work. Jay's paying you good money to jump yourself to death!"

Just before eight o'clock, Bob hurried to Byron's side and whispered something in the deejay's ear.

While a song played behind him, Byron turned up his microphone. "Okay, gang, time for a break. Why don't you all catch your breath and check out the door prizes?"

The word *prizes* buzzed through the gym and the kids outside hurried in from the hall. Again, Lillie knew she and Jay had done just the right things to make the jump-a-thon work.

"Our first prize is a twenty-five-dollar gift certificate from Papa's House," Byron announced. "Whoever gets this is going to make lots of friends." Laughter rippled through the crowd. "And the first winner is . . . ticket three-nine-eight!"

A freshman boy shoved his way to the front and handed his sweaty, crumpled ticket to Byron. The deejay made a production of peeling the paper off his palm and then wiping his wet hand on his pants leg. He said to the crowd, "If you don't mind, after this, you can just *show* me your tickets. I don't need to take them."

After handing out two more prizes, the deejay told them to resume jumping.

As Lillie jumped in the center of the gym, she noticed something strange. There seemed to be some kind of grapevine going on among the jumpers. One person would tell something to the next, who would tell the next person, and so on.

Lillie was curious. Was something going to happen that even she didn't know about yet? When the news reached her, a girl shouted in her ear, "They're giving away a TV! Don't leave!"

At eight-thirty, Byron used his electronic equipment to produce a drum roll. Then he moved to his mike. "We have to thank Ken's Appliances for this last door prize." Bob rolled a twenty-inch color TV onto the stage.

"Who will be the lucky winner?" Suspense music filled the air. Byron closed his eyes and fished in the ticket bucket. Pulling out a stub, he read, "Seven-zero-two!"

"It's me!" yelled a familiar voice.

"Not fair!" Several kids complained when Frank Lewis from the student council waved his ticket in the air.

"No sore losers," Byron said. "In fact, there are no losers at all. If you stick around, Sammy's Pizzaroo will be delivering thousands of pizzas at nine o'clock."

"All right!" The promise of food gave everyone new energy and restored their good humor.

Someone rested a hand on Lillie's shoulder. Hoping Jay had decided to stop by the gym, she said without turning around, "Checking up on me?"

But it was Bob Wilson. "Not really," he answered. "You did a great job, Lillie. Why don't you rest? You deserve it."

Lillie covered her disappointment with a grin. "I'd love to stop. My feet are killing me! But I've got too much money riding on this last twenty minutes to quit now."

"Did anyone I know sign your pledge sheet?" Bob asked.

Lillie wondered if he was really asking whether or not Jay had pledged for her. She wasn't about to tell him. "I've got a lot of names on my sheet, but there's still room for you."

Bob started walking away from her. "Thanks, but I've made enough pledges already."

"Are you ready to get out of here?" an exhausted Karin asked Lillie. It was close to nine-thirty.

"I didn't get any pizza yet," Lillie complained. She had been too busy thanking everyone for being part of the jump-a-thon to eat a bite.

"Pizza?" Karin laughed. "It's been gone since five after nine!"

Lillie's stomach growled. "I'm sorry to hear that." She sighed. "I really worked up an appetite."

"Maybe we can . . ."

But Lillie didn't hear a word her friend was saying. Jay had just walked into the gym. He looked great in his white T-shirt and faded jeans. Of course, he was also the only person she'd seen in two hours who wasn't hot and sweaty.

"Excuse me, Karin." She tried to smooth

down her damp hair as she hurried over to him.

"You're not jumping," he said when she reached him. He was trying hard not to smile.

"We're all done." She waved her arm, indicating the nearly empty gym. "The prizes are gone, Byron Hoddel has packed up his equipment, and the smallest jumpers are probably sound asleep at the shelter by now."

His dark gaze softened. "Did they have fun?"

Lillie smiled, remembering how the little kids had held their own competition. "They raced to see who could be the first to jump five times without getting the rope tangled around their ankles."

"I bet they all would have beat me."

She took a step back and stared at him. Had Jay Carson, Mr. Confident himself, actually just admitted there was something he couldn't do? "You said rope jumping wasn't *your kind of thing.* But that wasn't the real reason. You can't jump rope, can you?" she said accusingly.

"You're right, Lillie. I'm a fake." Jay didn't sound at all sorry for deceiving her, or for getting caught. He grinned.

So did Lillie. "Maybe I'll teach you how sometime, but not tonight. I'm too tired."

He glanced at her feet. "How do you feel?"

As soon as he asked, Lillie remembered how hungry she was. "I'm starving," she admitted.

"Maybe we could go somewhere," Jay suggested.

Lillie was about to accept his offer when Karin came up behind her, announcing, "We're all going to Sammy's."

"Who's 'we'?" Lillie asked.

"Everyone who's still here. Hey, you want to come, too?" Karin asked Jay.

He shook his head. "Uh, no thanks. I have to go somewhere else right now."

Lillie didn't believe a word of it. He had stayed away from the jump-a-thon so he wouldn't embarrass himself. And he had probably refused to go to Sammy's because he didn't want to spend too much time with a table full of mush-brains. Lillie angrily turned away.

But before she could join her friends, Jay touched her arm. "This is for you." He pushed an envelope into her hand, then strode away. He was gone before she pulled out the card. The cartoon on the front showed a girl with blond hair, big blue eyes . . . and enormous feet. Inside, he'd printed, *I'm sure you jumped for two full hours. I owe you eighty dollars. Don't worry, you'll get it tomorrow. But right now, go home and soak your feet.*

Lillie couldn't help grinning. Who would have guessed Jay could be so thoughtful?

"What's that?" Karin asked, peering at the card.

"A note from Jay." Lillie giggled. "He told me to go home and soak my feet."

Karin reached for the card. "Let me see it."

But Lillie tucked it in her pocket. "Nope."

"Then I'm not going to believe you." Karin pouted. "If crazy Jay Carson told one of us to soak anything, it would be our heads!"

Taking a deep breath, Lillie stood as tall as she could, all five feet five inches of her. "Think what you will, Karin Donovan. *I'm* going home to soak my feet . . . as soon as I eat half a pizza!"

"I've got to get out of here," Lillie told her friends at Sammy's an hour later. "I still have homework to do for tomorrow."

Bob Wilson groaned. "Me, too. Think anyone will take pity on us since we worked so hard tonight?"

"You might be able to talk *your* teachers into it," Karin said with a frown. "But I know Ms. Henderson will expect my math assignment to be done."

"Where *was* Ms. Henderson, anyway?" Lillie asked. "She helped with the jump-a-thon all week. I was sure she'd be there tonight."

"Me, too," Karin agreed.

Frank returned from getting another pitcher of soda for them. He looked very solemn. "You won't believe what I just heard. The teachers held a vote tonight—"

"A strike vote?" Lillie asked.

Frank nodded. "They said the school board stopped negotiating and they're not going to take it anymore."

"So did they vote to strike or not?" Bob demanded.

"Strike. And it starts tomorrow!"

Everybody at the table whooped with joy. Karin rocked back in her chair. "I'm going to sleep till noon tomorrow. And when I finally wake up, I won't have to worry about my math assignment!"

Chapter Five

"I never thought running a business would be so easy," Karin exclaimed on Monday morning. Karin and Lillie were in the park, surrounded by small children.

"*Easy?*" Lillie struggled to remove her leg from a child's iron grip. It had seemed like a good idea to start a babysitting service during the strike. After all, there were lots of working parents with kids who could not stay home alone. But there were more children than she and Karin had ever expected.

"Maybe you're right. It's not so easy," Karin admitted as little Tommy Porter jumped on her back. Tommy would only be staying with them until two o'clock each day. The only problem was surviving until then. They couldn't stay in the park the entire time.

"And it's only our first day." Lillie groaned.

"Okay, gang," Karin told the kids. "Here are the rules: No pushing, shoving, or fighting. No one leaves the sand pit area in the playground without permission. And *no throwing sand!* We will be watching you! Got it?"

Tommy raised his hand. "Will my mom find me here?"

"Don't worry, Tommy. We'll take care of everything," Karin promised. "Any more questions?"

A blond kindergarten-age girl named Abby raised her hand. "I have to go to the bathroom."

"Lillie will help you." Abby trotted up to Lillie while Karin told the others, "Okay. On your mark . . . get set . . . go!"

The kids screamed all the way from the sidewalk to the monkey bars.

"The next time someone asks what you want to do when you get out of school," Lillie said to her friend, "consider joining the army. You'd fit right in, Sergeant Donovan!"

When Lillie returned with Abby, Karin was sitting on a park bench where she could watch all five of their charges on the climber. Abby followed Lillie to the bench.

"Lillie," she whined, "it's time for my nap."

"Nap?" Lillie turned to Karin for a consultation. They hadn't anticipated that any of their clients would still take naps.

"Why don't you just lay your head on my lap and close your eyes?" Karin suggested.

Lillie thought that was very nice of her friend until she realized that Karin now had an excuse not to chase after any of the other children. "Smooth move," she told her partner.

"Why are you so crabby?" Karin asked. "Haven't you heard from Jay, the nut job who told you to go soak your . . . feet?"

Lillie blushed. "We were just working together on the jump-a-thon. Why should he call me?" Lillie hoped she was convincing her friend.

Actually, she *had* expected Jay to call her after the strike started. She missed stopping by his locker and wondering if he might be waiting for her in the morning. But it seemed as if the saying "Out of sight, out of mind" was very true when it came to Jay Carson.

"Do you hear what I hear?" Karin asked softly, since Abby was trying to rest.

"It sounds like b-o-y-s."

Lillie stood to have a better view of the park. "You're right, Karin. They're everywhere."

"Really?" Her friend glanced at the little girl in her lap and sighed with resignation. "What are they doing?"

Lillie pointed to a field beyond the monkey bars. "The Newton High baseball team is practicing over there. . . ." Then she glanced behind the bench. "And the cross-country team seems to be taking laps around the whole park."

"It's kind of sad, isn't it?" Karin gently stroked Abby's soft hair. "The teams can't even practice with their coaches, and they can't play any league games until the strike is over."

"I wish the school board had given the teachers what they wanted." Lillie knew her father hated being away from his classes. He enjoyed teaching, but now he had to spend most of his time at union meetings.

"Tommy's throwing sand at the girls," Karin announced.

"I'm on my way," Lillie called over her shoulder as she charged toward the sand pit. "Tommy Porter, stop throwing sand *this instant*!"

Tommy froze in mid-throw, the sand sifting through his chubby fingers. Lillie squatted so she was at eye level with the boy. "You can't make friends by throwing sand in people's faces."

"I don't want them to be my friends. They're just chicken girls," he told her with authority.

"Then you shouldn't pay any attention to them at all," Lillie suggested.

"You gonna tell my mom that I was so bad

you don't want me back?" Tommy's lower lip began to tremble.

"Of course we want you back," Lillie fibbed. A little white lie was better than ruining a child's self-image, wasn't it? On the other hand, her own esteem wouldn't be shaken if Tommy didn't like her. With a hint of hope in her voice, she added, "Unless you don't want to come back tomorrow."

"I do!" He threw his arms around her neck and refused to release her. "I *hate* it when people don't let me come back!"

She hugged him for a moment. "I'd like to have you come back tomorrow."

He threw back his arms and honored her with a gap-toothed grin. "Okay. I'm gonna climb now!"

"I'll watch." Lillie stood with her arms folded in front of her.

"Having fun?" a deep male voice inquired.

Lillie knew it was Jay even before she turned around and found herself staring into his chest—or more accurately, at the third snap on his leather jacket. "What are you doing here?"

He lifted a pen and sketch pad. "Sketching."

"Cartoons?" She tried to peek at his work, hoping to see his next piece for the *Newton News*.

"I try to come to the park at least once a week just to watch people. I usually see something I want to draw."

"Really?" Lillie shaded her eyes, to make sure all five of the children were still in sight.

"What are *you* doing here?" Jay asked. "Watching the baseball team work out? Or is it the track team?"

Lillie gasped when one of the kids started to lose her grip on the monkey bars. To Lillie's amazement, it was Tommy who reached out to help in the nick of time.

With a grin, she said to Jay, "You think I'm watching guys?"

He studied Lillie, trying to read her expression. "Maybe," he said finally. "Maybe you *are* looking for some social action."

Lillie shook her head. "Wrong. Karin and I have started a babysitting service, and I'm going crazy after just one day!" She sighed. "And the day isn't even half over yet!"

"You're working?" He sounded more surprised than Lillie thought he should be.

"Did you think I'd sleep until noon every day?" What *did* Jay think of her, anyway?

He shrugged. "I'm not sure what I thought."

Great. He probably hadn't thought about her at all since the strike started.

Jay went on, "I imagined you tanning by some pool."

"Tanning?" Lillie pulled down her sweater sleeves to cover her wrists. "It's not *that* warm. When did we ever have tanning weather in May in Minnesota? Where did you grow up— Arizona?"

"Actually, I'm originally from New York," he told her seriously.

That was an interesting bit of information. "When did you move to Middleton?"

"When I was three."

Lillie was just about to scold him for teasing her when a small voice said, "Lillie, I need a hug."

It was Monica, a little redheaded girl who had a green stain on her shirt. Lillie smiled and picked up the child. "I just happen to have an extra hug right here."

"You look pretty busy. I'll see you later," Jay said, turning to walk away. Lillie gazed after him. What did *later* mean? Later that day? That week? That year?

"Time to hit the road," Karin told the kids when Abby woke up from her nap. "Tommy's mom will be coming to pick him up soon, and we don't want to miss Tommy's mom."

The other children said eagerly, "No, we sure don't!" The boy Tommy had just tried to wrestle to the ground sounded especially eager.

Lillie lagged behind, pretending she was watching for any stragglers. All five of the children were lined up behind Karin.

"Uh . . . Lillie?" Jay didn't exactly run to catch up with her, but he did move faster than usual. "I know you don't have much time, but I have something for you." He handed her a page from his sketch pad. On it was a drawing of her playing with one of the children. He had caught her goofy expression perfectly, though she hadn't realized she had made such a silly face.

"Thank you," Lillie said happily. "I'm going to get a frame for it. Did you sign it?"

He pointed to the scribbled signature in the lower right-hand corner. Suddenly he asked, "Would you like to go see *The Long Voyage* with me tomorrow night?"

Lillie had heard of the film. It was a long story of immigrants, acted in a foreign language with subtitles. Although she didn't usually enjoy serious movies, she knew she'd gladly watch anything at all if she could do it with Jay. What could she say but yes?

Chapter Six

Lillie tugged the pale pink shirt over her head and threw it on her bed. Something sweet and pastel just wouldn't be right for a movie about starving immigrants. What *would* be appropriate? What kind of girls did Jay usually date? Did they wear leather jackets and torn jeans? Did they wear lots of makeup, or no makeup at all? She'd never seen Jay with a girl. What was she going to do?

"How are you coming along?" her mother called from the bottom of the stairs.

"Help!" Lillie cried.

Mary Evans came upstairs and gazed at the clothes scattered all over the room. "Is there a problem?"

"I can't get dressed!"

"A really big date, huh?" her mother asked.

"Yes. No. I don't know." How could Lillie explain her feelings about Jay to her mother? She couldn't even explain them to herself. She liked being with him, and she wanted to get to know him better. But did that mean this was a *big* date?

"Your father says that Jay isn't like the other boys you know."

So her parents had been talking about him. Lillie explained, "It's not like I'm trying to *impress* Jay. I just don't want to wear something totally wrong."

Mrs. Evans sat down on the bed. "What kind of boy is he?"

It was a difficult question, but Lillie did her best to answer it. "He's really involved in things like politics and the environment. He wears a leather jacket most of the time and his hair's kind of long. And he wears an ear stud. He's . . . well, *different*."

"I see." But Lillie wasn't convinced her mother had a good mental picture of Jay from her description, until her mother said, "He's not the type to appreciate cute and perky."

"Exactly!"

"I think I know just what you need."

Lillie started to worry. What would she do if her mother rushed to her studio downstairs and whipped up some weird outfit for her date?

But Mrs. Evans was rummaging through the clothes strewn across Lillie's bed. She held up a pale blue cotton sweater and a pair of jeans. "These should do it."

"You think so?" Lillie asked dubiously. It seemed like such a plain choice for her mother, the designer, to make.

"The sweater makes your eyes look even bluer. And this pair of jeans makes you look even slimmer than usual."

Mrs. Evans waited while Lillie slipped the sweater over her head, and helped her brush her long, blond hair. "Mmm . . . you smell good." Mrs. Evans sniffed appreciatively.

"It's supposed to be wildflowers." Lillie had thought Jay might appreciate something natural.

She put on the jeans and held her breath while she zipped them up. Then she reached for the locket on her dresser and slipped the chain around her neck. "Do I look okay?"

Her mother stood back to get a full view. "The clothes are right, but you look like you're going to school." She tapped her chin with her finger. "I think you need to do something with your hair."

Lillie walked over to her mirror. "I've got an

67

idea." With her mother's help, she French braided her hair. But she couldn't decide how to cover the elastic band at the bottom of the braid. Her favorite pink polka-dot bow would probably make Jay gag.

"I've got just what you need downstairs. Hold it right there."

Lillie waited patiently while her mother searched in her studio. Mrs. Evans had been right about the clothes. She'd probably be right about Lillie's hair, too.

But Lillie's confidence was shaken when her mother arrived with a piece of fabric and a pair of scissors in her hand. Her worst fears were confirmed. Her mother was going to *create* something.

"Don't make that face at me," her mother scolded. "I know better than to try anything experimental on you."

She snipped out a thin strip of blue printed cloth, which she then twisted into a cord. Then she stood behind Lillie and wrapped the cloth around the elastic band and neatly tucked the ends out of sight.

"I didn't know you could do that!" Lillie exclaimed. "Thanks, Mom!" She'd seen tricks like that in fashion magazines, but she had never been able to make them work on her own.

The doorbell rang and Lillie jumped. He was here. She was going on a real date with Jay Carson. It was wonderful, but what would they talk about after the movie? She hoped Jay wouldn't want to spend the whole evening discussing the social signifcance of the film. If he did, she was afraid she'd look like an idiot.

Her father was talking with Jay in the living room when she came downstairs. Lillie saw that Jay's jacket was open to show his green SAVE THE WHALES T-shirt. Somehow, it was reassuring that he hadn't gotten dressed up. He looked just the way she'd expected him to.

"Well, Jay," her father was saying, "Lillie's curfew is midnight since there's no school tomorrow."

"But I'll be home earlier than that, unfortunately. I've got to face those *kids* in the morning!" Lillie groaned. "I'd rather go to school!"

"I'll remind you that you said that when this strike is settled," her mother teased.

"Ugh. Let's not talk about the strike," Lillie said. Thinking about the baseball team and the runners she had seen at the park, she added, "Everyone is losing."

"I hope it ends soon, for everybody's sake," Jay declared.

Lillie's father agreed. "We all want to get back to our routines. But the talks have stalled. There's going to be a demonstration on Friday in front of the district office of the Board of Ed."

"I've heard about it," Jay said. "I might go."

Of course he will, Lillie thought. With his interest in politics, she didn't think anyone could keep Jay Carson home on demonstration day.

"I hate to seem rude or anything," Jay said, "but the movie starts in fifteen minutes."

"Then I guess you two should be leaving." Mrs. Evans gave Lillie a kiss on the cheek. "Have fun."

Everyone seemed to feel great about her date except Lillie. Her palms were cold and clammy. Before she left, she whispered to her mother, "Wish me luck!"

"How did you like the movie?" Jay asked as they left the theater two hours later.

Lillie hesitated. It had been interesting. She supposed she'd learned something. But it was hard to *like* two hours of subtitles.

"What did *you* think about it?" she inquired, trying to avoid committing herself.

He chuckled. "I guess you're more used to seeing big Hollywood films, right?"

Lillie flushed. She didn't want him to think she was superficial. "Yes . . . but that doesn't mean I didn't enjoy tonight," she said truthfully. After all, she had been sitting next to Jay in the dark for two whole hours. She had hoped he would hold her hand or stretch his arm across the back of her seat, but he hadn't.

Did that mean he liked her only as a friend? Maybe he didn't hold hands on a first date—if this was really a date. Maybe they were just two people who had gone to a movie together. Jay Carson was so different from the rest of the guys Lillie knew that it was hard to know how to interpret his actions.

"You're pretty quiet," he said when he held the car door open for her.

"Mmm . . ." Lillie wondered if she should pretend she had been analyzing the film's deeper meaning.

Inside the car, Jay switched on the overhead light for a moment and checked his watch. "Ten-fifteen. Do you want to go somewhere else, or would you rather go home?"

"I don't have to be home until midnight."

"But you need to rest up for those kids in the morning," he reminded her.

What did he want her to say? What did he

want? Did he want to spend more time with her? Or did he want to drop her off on her doorstep? Not knowing if she'd ever get another chance to be with Jay again—they wouldn't have any reason to see each other at school after the strike was settled—Lillie decided to take matters into her own hands.

"Let's go somewhere." She leaned back in her seat. "Take me someplace where we can have fun."

Jay switched on the radio and tapped out the musical beat on the steering wheel. "Something fun."

Lillie tried to recognize the song on the radio while Jay did his thinking. He definitely wasn't tuned in to WXYZ. "What station is this?"

"KPMJ," he told her. "They play oldies."

"Like the Beatles?" she asked. She didn't know anything about Jay's taste in music.

"A lot of the songs from the sixties are about justice and equality. I like the messages."

"I see." And she did. Those were the things that interested him.

Jay shifted the car into gear, and then drove out of the parking lot and turned onto a city street. "I thought the movie was very well done." He turned down the volume on the radio. "It gave me a lot to think about. My grandfather was an immigrant." Jay stared straight ahead as he spoke. "I bet he came to America about the same time as Gus in the movie. But from what I've heard, my dad's father wasn't as forgiving as old Gus. By the time he died, he had disinherited four of his six children."

Lillie stared at him in surprise. She thought cranky old men only disinherited their kids in novels.

"Well, he had his reasons," Jay said a little defensively.

Lillie hurried to agree with him. "I'm sure he did."

"My Grandfather Cullivan Carson truly loved his new country, and he was hurt when his children didn't share his feelings. One moved to Canada rather than enlist in the army. Another seemed to think that crime *did* pay. I forget exactly what the others did. . . ."

"But *your* father didn't disappoint his dad." Lillie could see how Cullivan had affected both C. J. Carson and Jay. That was probably one of the reasons why Jay was so different from the other kids at Newton.

Jay stopped at a red light. "Just think, Lillie, my grandfather came here from Ireland with only a few dollars in his pocket. But he saved enough money to send my father to law school, and now C. J. Carson is known all around the United States. Where else in the world do you think that could happen?"

"Nowhere, I guess," Lillie said as they crossed the intersection.

Jay nodded. "Darn right. What about your family, Lillie? Where did they come from originally?"

She took a few minutes to review the few stories she'd heard at home. "My mother's parents came from Sweden, just like in the movie. But no one talks about what happened when they first got to this country."

"You should try to find out," Jay said. "It helps you appreciate what you have."

"Oh, I do. I like living in Middleton and going to Newton High. But my family's story isn't quite as impressive as yours."

"What do you mean?"

"You know my father's a history teacher. And my mother designs strange clothes," she told him. "It's not quite like being a famous attorney who fights for people's rights."

"Your father is a great teacher," Jay said, to her surprise. "He actually makes history come alive for his students. They don't realize how much they're learning. Don't ever think he's not important."

Lillie was silent. She loved her dad, but she

had never thought of him as a very important person. Jay certainly had some interesting ideas.

He turned left on a side street Lillie didn't recognize and asked, "So, are you going to look into your family's past?"

"This is starting to sound like homework," she teased.

"Don't tell me I've been lecturing you." He sighed. "My mother says I do that all the time at home, but I sure didn't want to do it to you, Lillie."

Her heart skipped a beat. He was worried he had bored her! "Don't apologize. You've given me a lot to think about."

"Good." Jay grinned.

Lillie touched the chain around her neck. Until now, her only tie with her grandmother had been the locket she always wore. Now suddenly she wanted to know more about the people whose solemn photographs were hidden inside it.

She blinked when Jay drove into a brightly lit parking lot and said, "We're here."

"*Skate Center?* You want to go roller skating?"

"Why not?" Jay's grin was a dare. "You said you'd like to have some fun."

"But I thought you'd take me to The Dive or

Sammy's Pizzaroo . . ." She hated to think of making a fool of herself on roller skates.

"You're hungry? I hear the hot dogs at the snack bar are great." With his hand on the car keys, as if he wasn't sure whether or not they should stay, Jay said, "Wait a minute. Don't you skate? Are you worried about falling down or something?"

"Me?" Lillie held her head high. "I'm a good roller skater—or at least I used to be when I was little."

"Then what are we waiting for?" He hopped out of the car and came over to open Lillie's door. "I was city roller skating champion when I was in junior high."

Jay Carson a skating champion? He certainly was full of surprises. "You're kidding!"

He grinned as he took Lillie's hand and pulled her out of the car. "I think you're just stalling. Come on—I'll prove it to you."

Chapter Seven

Lillie rocked back on her heels to admire her own work. In big black letters her picket sign now said: WHAT'S AN EDUCATION WORTH? PAY OUR TEACHERS FAIRLY!

Workers were scattered all around the Wilsons' family room Wednesday night. The demonstration was going to happen in two days, and Bob expected all the members of the student council to participate.

Across the room, Bob had his little sister drawing the front doors of Newton High with huge locks on them, and he was busy supervising everyone's projects.

He stopped next to Frank and read his placard: END THE STRIKE. WE WANT TO LEARN. Frank laughed and said, "I want to learn, but I also want to graduate."

The other seniors in the room cheered in agreement.

"Will we have to go to school longer to make up for the time we're losing?" one girl asked.

"I hope not," Karin said. "I'm supposed to start my summer job at the mall the second week of June."

Bob voiced what was on all their minds when he stated, "We have to make the school board start talking to the teachers again. It's up to them to get this thing solved!"

"Hopefully the demonstration will get the message across," Lillie told him with a yawn.

"Partying too late?" Bob joked. "That's one way to enjoy the strike."

Lillie shook her head. "Believe me, there haven't been any parties. Karin and I are running a babysitting service for kids with working parents."

"How hard can that be?" Bob asked.

Karin chuckled. "You should try it some-time! We have this little demon called Tommy. Since it was raining this morning, we thought finger painting would be a good indoor acti-vity—"

"Until Tommy started painting one of the kids," Lillie finished. It had taken her almost half an hour to get the paint out of the little girl's hair.

"But why are *you* so tired, Lillie?" one of the girls asked. "I don't notice Karin yawning and falling asleep over her picket sign."

Lillie just shrugged. She wasn't going to announce to the world that she'd been roller skating with Jay until twelve-fifteen the previous night. Her parents had been slightly upset that she was late, but it had been worth it.

Who would have believed Jay was an expert skater? While she'd been making a few respectable moves on wheels, he was spinning and jumping. Heads turned. The colored lights lit up his ear stud, and his hair had blown freely behind him as he sped around the rink.

And she hadn't needed to fall to get some help from him. He had volunteered to give her a few pointers, and he hadn't hesitated to slide his arm around her during the lesson, either. Remembering that, Lillie smiled.

"What's Lillie grinning about?" Frank wanted to know, turning to Karin for an explanation. But Karin couldn't tell him much. Lillie was too confused about her feelings to talk to her friend about him.

"Forget Lillie," Bob told them. "Let's get back to business. Who has some ideas for picketing chants?"

"We want our teachers back!" Frank suggested.

Bob and some of the others gave it a try. "We want our teachers back! We want our teachers back!"

"It needs a little something more," Karin said. "Something punchier."

Lillie got an idea. "What about, 'We want English! We want Math! We want all our teachers back!' "

"I *hate* math," one of the girls cried.

"But what other subject even comes close to rhyming with *back*?" Lillie asked.

"How about *track*?" a boy suggested, but he was shouted down.

They practiced yelling Lillie's chant as loud as they could until Bob's mother asked them to keep it down.

"We can't say the same thing the whole time," Bob told the would-be picketers.

"I'm sure the teachers have some plans of their own," Karin said.

"Are we the only students who will be marching with the teachers?" Frank asked. "Or are other kids making signs somewhere else?"

Lillie told him, "Most of the kids are probably thrilled to have an unscheduled vacation, just the way we were at first. We might be the only ones on the teachers' side."

"But think how much they've helped us," a girl said earnestly. "Ms. Henderson always has time for student council projects— "

Karin interrupted. "Not to mention tutoring me after school so I could pass math last year."

"Don't forget that Lillie's dad is a teacher, too. That means we're doing this for him," Frank added, and the others agreed.

"I guess we won't know who else will be there until Friday morning. Still, in case there aren't any other students, we should be ready. Anybody got another idea for a chant?" Bob inquired.

"Does it have to rhyme?" Frank asked. "If it doesn't, we could just keep repeating, 'Free our school! Free our school!' "

"I like it," Lillie exclaimed. She thought it matched the picture that Bob's sister had drawn on the picket sign. Although there really wasn't a huge lock chained to the Newton doors, there might as well have been. She couldn't even get her books out of her locker to finish the English assignment that would have been due the next day, and Lillie really loved English.

"What else do we need to do tonight?" Karin asked.

"I think we're ready," Bob declared. "Everybody be sure to wear comfortable shoes and bring your signs with you on Friday. Nine A.M. sharp, in front of the Board of Ed. Office."

Lillie wondered if Jay would show up at the demonstration with his friend Lucas. He'd told her he might come. Maybe he'd call her tomorrow and she could ask him. It would be fun to spend Friday morning marching next to Jay Carson.

"It's great to have you come along, Gina," Lillie told her friend on the way to the park the next day.

"Tommy! Cut that out!" Karin shouted.

Gina laughed. "You're just happy to have one more body along to keep these wild kids under control."

"That's not true, exactly," Lillie protested as they reached the park.

Mandy tugged on Gina's hand. "Gina? I have to go to the bathroom."

Gina raised one eyebrow at Lillie and sighed. "Point me in the right direction—I don't know where the restrooms are."

Tommy and the other children settled down to building a city in the sand. Lillie watched him taking charge, telling the smaller ones what to do. She turned to Karin, grinning. "I just had a funny thought! Who does Tommy remind you of?"

Karin observed Tommy ordering the others where to put the town's streets and houses. Her dark eyes sparkled. "Bob Wilson?"

"Yeah." Lillie grimaced. "It's kind of scary knowing there's a little one warming up to tell the world how to behave."

"A little what?" Gina asked after she had left Mandy with the other busy town builders.

"We've decided that Tommy is a clone of Bob Wilson," Lillie told her.

"Bob's not so bad," Gina said. "Doesn't he keep the student council running smoothly?"

"That's because he never gives anyone a chance to screw things up. He tells everybody what to do and then makes sure they do it. Take Lillie, for example," Karin said. "She didn't want to work with Jay Carson on the jump-a-thon project, but Bob practically forced her into it."

Lillie smile a little. It was hard to believe she had actually been nervous about working with Jay two weeks ago.

"The jump-a-thon was the student council's most successful promotion," Gina pointed out. "We made lots of money for the homeless kids."

"Yeah, I know. What I'm trying to say is—"

Gina glanced over Karin's shoulder. "Speak of the devil!"

"What? Bob's here?" Karin asked.

"Not Bob," Gina whispered. "Jay Carson!"

Lillie jumped when two strong hands squeezed her shoulders.

"What's wrong, Lillie?" he asked. "Are you still sore from Tuesday night?"

Gina and Karin stared at him, then at Lillie, obviously wondering what Jay was talking about. Realizing that he had a very curious audience, Jay suggested to Lillie that they take a walk.

"Do you guys mind?" Lillie's friends were still speechless, but they nodded when she asked, "Will you be all right if I take a break for a few minutes?"

Jay touched her elbow. "Let's go."

They walked toward the swimming pool, which wouldn't open for another month. Jay said quietly, "You didn't tell them about going to the movie with me, did you?"

"No."

"Are you ashamed of me?"

Lillie looked up at him, blue eyes wide. "Oh, no! Not at all, Jay."

"Then why don't you want them to know we're . . . friends?"

"Is that what we are?" That was one of the

reasons Lillie hadn't discussed Jay with the others. She wasn't sure how to explain what was going on between them.

Jay sat on a bench and pulled her down beside him. He didn't release her hand when he said, "Until we worked on that project together, I didn't know how much fun I could have with—"

"A mush-brain?" she teased.

"I feel pretty stupid for thinking you didn't care about important things," he admitted. "I've learned a lot from you."

"Like what?" Jay seemed to know so much more about the world than she did. Lillie couldn't imagine what she could possibly have taught him.

"Well, for one thing, that people don't have to look and act like me—or Lucas—to be involved."

"And I've learned that people who look and act like you and Lucas aren't necessarily strange," Lillie said, smiling. She thought about Jay's friend with the red bandanna on his head. "What's Lucas interested in?"

Jay chuckled. "Right now, he's obsessed with plastic. He's convinced we'll all be buried under tons of plastic garbage by the year 2000."

"And you don't think so?" Lillie was surprised to hear Jay almost making fun of an ecological issue.

"Of course it's important. But Lucas . . ." Jay paused. "Well, Lucas uses some weird ways to make his points. I can express my concerns in my cartoon strip, but he does *other* things."

"Like what?" Lillie suddenly pictured Lucas trying to sabotage a plastics factory, but Jay had a less dramatic story.

"For instance, last week he brought his own plate to a fast food restaurant, handed it over the counter, and ordered a burger to go—because he's opposed to those Styrofoam carry-out containers."

"He must have confused the person on the other side of the counter," Lillie said between giggles. She wished she could have been there.

"It is kind of funny," Jay agreed. "I'd like to put it in my next cartoon strip . . . if the *Newton News* ever goes back into production, that is."

"When do you think the teachers' strike will be over?" Lillie asked.

With a hint of sarcasm, Jay said, "You should know better than I. Your dad's a teacher."

Lillie ignored his tone, assuming he was frustrated by the strike. Everyone was. "He goes to meetings every day, and each night he comes home discouraged."

"What do you think about tomorrow's demonstration?"

"I'll be there. My mom's going to cover the babysitting service for Karin and me," Lillie said. She wondered how many students shared their interest in the demonstration. "I suppose a lot of kids would think it's stupid to get involved. They'd say it's the *teachers'* problem, not ours."

"Who cares?" Jay said. "I think it's great you're standing up for your beliefs. Everyone's entitled to his—or her—own opinion. But what about the teachers? Do *they* have the right to strike?"

"Of course!"

"But what about their obligation to their students?" Jay almost sounded angry.

Lillie tried hard to understand where he was coming from. Why was he arguing with her?

"You have to be able to answer questions like that if you want to support your cause," he said.

"I see," she replied. He had just been testing her, challenging her to think. Lillie decided to consider the question so she could answer it the next time someone asked her.

Suddenly they both heard children yelling. Lillie sighed. "I guess I should get back to work."

"I'll walk with you."

Jay didn't say much as they covered the short distance back to the playground, where they found Karin having a heart-to-heart with Tommy while Gina dried a few children's tears.

Jay squeezed her hand. "It looks like they need you. I'll see you tomorrow."

"Another day is over. And we survived!" Lillie declared later that day after the last child left with his mother. "Want a snack?"

Lillie and her friends went into the kitchen. She found three diet sodas in the fridge and brought them to the table.

"Don't think we're going to forget what happened today just because you're being nice to us," Karin teased.

"Really! I'm not leaving this house until you tell us *all* about Jay Carson," Gina added.

"Tell us about Tuesday night," Karin urged.

"We went to a movie and then we went roller skating," Lillie said casually.

"Roller skating? *Jay Carson?*" Gina hooted.

Lillie laughed, too. "That's what I thought until he put on his skates. He was city champion in junior high, and he skates really well."

"No kidding!" Karin stared in disbelief.

"You didn't see him skate. It was amazing!" Lillie grinned, remembering how Jay had been the center of attention and seemed to love every minute of it.

"So, are you two a couple or what?" Gina asked, getting to the heart of the matter.

"A couple?" Lillie shook her soda can and listened to the remaining liquid fizz inside. "I'm not sure. . . ."

"Oh, come on!" As the most experienced dater in the group, Gina took charge. "He takes you to a movie and then he tries to impress you with his secret talent. And *then* he comes to the park to see you."

Lillie wasn't convinced. "It doesn't mean anything. Boys have done more than that for you and you didn't become a couple."

"But we're talking about *Jay Carson!*" Gina was firm. "I've never seen Jay with anyone except that guy with the red bandanna. I always figured that if he had a girlfriend, she'd wear leather and ride a motorcycle. I'm amazed he can appreciate a nice, normal person like you, Lillie."

"It's interesting being with him," Lillie admitted. "He's definitely not like other guys we know."

"Is that all you're going to tell us?" Karin sounded disappointed.

Lillie shrugged. "Sorry. But there's no more to tell."

However, there were many more questions that Lillie kept asking herself. Did she want to be more than Jay's friend? Did he want to be more than just a friend to her? Gina was right—it seemed hard to believe Jay would really want to get involved with "a nice, normal person" like her.

And Lillie wasn't convinced she could deal with someone like Jay. She knew what to expect from the kind of boys she and her friends usually dated, but she didn't know the rules when it came to Jay Carson. Maybe there weren't any rules at all. Was she ready for that?

Chapter Eight

"Isn't Johnny staying?" Karin called to Gina when she hopped out of the red sports car on Friday morning.

Gina grinned as her boyfriend sped away from the Middleton School Administration Building. "He was willing to jump rope for me, but he's drawn the line at picketing. He doesn't ever want to go back to school!"

"Well, it looks like a lot of kids do." Karin shaded her eyes from the sun as their friends arrived with picket signs in hand.

"You sure look great," Lillie told Gina. Her petite friend, could wear the trendiest clothes with style, even the purple cotton harem-style pants she had on.

Gina smoothed down the extra cloth over her thighs. "Do you recognize these?"

Both the other girls said, "No . . ."

"They came from your mother's shop, Lillie," Gina said. "Why haven't you ever worn anything like this to school?"

Lillie laughed. "Because I'd look like a hippo in pants puffed out like that!"

"She'd rather wear her comfortable old Newton sweatshirt," Karin observed.

"And what's wrong with it?" Lillie pushed up the sleeves of her blue and white top. It was a sunny morning, but the temperature was cool. And not knowing exactly how to dress at her first demonstration, she wanted to be comfortable. Who needed to worry about clothes at a time like this?

"Don't make fun of Lillie's sweatshirt," Gina reproached her friend. "Check out her hair. I wish I could do that with mine."

Lillie did a pirouette to show off her twin ponytails that bounced up and down when she moved. "You could if you wanted to. You've got much more manageable hair than mine."

Karin toyed with her red plastic hoop earrings. "Isn't anyone going to notice my new fashion purchase?"

"They're definitely you," Gina said with a smile.

"Are you guys ready?" Bob asked, coming up behind Gina and tugging on her long braid.

Karin whispered, "Just what Tommy Porter would do."

Lillie's hand flew up to her mouth to try to smother her giggles, but she failed.

Bob frowned at her. "Can't you be serious, Lillie? We're here to convince the school board to solve this disaster."

"Yeah, Lillie," Gina teased in a tough voice. "Shape up or I'll hit you over the head with this sign."

Bob's sister had had so much fun making signs that she had continued to work after the others had gone home on Wednesday night. Gina had one of the new ones. It said:

I EVEN MISS MY TRIGONOMETRY CLASS. HELP!

Bob sighed in disgust. "Good thing we're not depending on the three of you to settle the strike."

"Lighten up," Gina told him.

"The teachers are coming," Lillie said as a group of adults came toward them from the parking lot.

"There's your dad," Karin said.

Lillie waved at her father and stood on her toes to get a better look. "Ms. Henderson is here, too."

Gina rested her sign on her shoulder. "It's great to see everyone again."

The demonstrators began to get organized.

As Lillie and her friends joined the teachers, another half dozen students approached. She hoped there would be enough kids to make an impression on the school board. They had to understand the teachers weren't the only ones who wanted a settlement.

Ms. Henderson clapped her hands and all conversations hushed. "It's great to see so many of you today. We all want to thank the students who have come out to support us. We'll be marching on the sidewalk outside the main entrance so anyone coming into or out of the building will have to notice us."

The students joined the teachers and began marching in a circle. Lillie had to take a little time to get organized. First, she put her sign over her left shoulder and nearly hit Karin on the nose. Things worked much better when she held the placard over her right shoulder.

"I thought you said we were going to chant," Gina said from behind Karin.

"I guess we're waiting for Bob to start," Karin said.

"Why do we have to wait for him?" Gina asked.

"Beats me," Karin said. Then she added, "Let's do yours, Lillie. One . . . two . . . three . . ."

The two girls started to chant. "We want

English. We want math. We want all our teachers back!"

The teachers chuckled as the other students joined in loudly. Those kids who weren't carrying picket signs began to clap their hands to the beat.

Lillie noticed a Channel Four news truck pull up and park along the sidewalk. A reporter hurried out of the van, followed by a man with a video camera. The teachers pointed her toward Ms. Henderson, who was acting as the demonstration leader.

As Lillie passed the two women, she heard Ms. Henderson saying, "We teachers are responsible for educating the voters, the workers, the politicians of tomorrow. But we are paid less than middle managers in industry. . . ."

Living with a teacher, Lillie had heard all these points of view before. But she hoped the people of Middleton, including members of the school board, would listen to Ms. Henderson on the news that night and take action.

"Psst! Lillie!"

"What, Gina?" she asked.

"Where's Jay? I'd have thought this would be just his kind of thing."

Lillie shrugged. "I thought he would be here, too. I wonder what's happened to him." Had he gone to the school, not realizing that everyone was meeting at the administration building? Or maybe he thought they weren't going to start picketing until later in the day.

Frank led the next round of yelling with the enthusiasm of a cheerleader, which made Gina giggle. "Free our school! Free our school!"

The cameraman who'd been filming Ms. Henderson turned now and focused on the marchers. Lillie heard him tell the reporter, "Let's stick around for a while and see if anything interesting happens."

Then Lillie saw another group of people with signs coming toward them from across the street. Karin asked, "More marchers?"

"I hope so," Lillie said.

But when the newcomers lifted their signs, Lillie and her friends read them and gasped. They said things like, MY TAXES ARE ALREADY HIGH ENOUGH and TEACHERS WHO STRIKE ARE HURTING OUR CHILDREN.

"How can they?" Gina asked in amazement.

Lillie couldn't answer. She had never imagined that anyone might oppose them. The new group didn't form a circle and march. They just stood together and held their signs up in silent protest.

Bob suddenly started to shout in his loudest voice, "We want English! We want math! . . ."

96

As each person passed by the silent protesters, they were careful to turn their signs so the others could read them.

As Lillie came around the circle, she angled her PAY OUR TEACHERS WHAT THEY'RE WORTH sign toward the woman who declared her taxes were too high. But she nearly dropped her placard altogether when she saw who was standing behind the woman.

"What's he doing over *there*?" Gina hissed.

That was the exact question buzzing through Lillie's head. Why was *Jay Carson* standing with the people who wanted the teachers to give up their demands and go back to their schools? At least he didn't have an offensive sign. His hands were buried deep in his jacket pockets.

"I never thought Jay would side with the establishment," Karin said in amazement. "He's such a rebel!"

"I know." But Lillie knew Jay was much too smart to be confused. He was not standing in that crowd by mistake. She was stunned. They had discussed the strike. They had agreed it was a bad thing and that it should end soon. Had she missed some sign that should have told her they thought that for completely different reasons? Lillie had expected to march *with* Jay, not to see him standing with a group of unfriendly protesters. Suddenly she felt too miserable to join in the chant. It was obvious that she didn't understand Jay Carson at all.

"There's a water cooler on the edge of the parking lot," Karin told the others as she slipped back into her place in line after a short break.

"I could use a drink," Lillie admitted.

Gina said, "You go next, Lillie. I'll march for both of us while you're gone."

Lillie didn't argue. She was dying of thirst. After she had handed her sign to a student who didn't have one, she headed toward the parking lot, where a table had been set up with water and paper cups. But when she got there, Lillie stopped dead in her tracks. Jay Carson was standing at the table, smiling and holding a cup of water out to her. Lillie didn't want to take it from him, but her dry throat didn't leave her any choice. She took the cup and muttered, "Thank you."

"Are you mad at me?" he asked when she glared at him over the rim of her paper cup.

"Mad?" she repeated. "Why should I be mad? I'm delighted that my *friend*, a person who I thought agreed with me about the strike, thinks the teachers are wrong!"

"Can't friends disagree?" Jay said quietly.

Lillie had to admit that he had a point. She didn't get ruffled every time she and Karin had different opinions. But that was different. Jay had tricked her. "I didn't know there would be two groups here, but obviously you did. How could you say you might see me today when you knew we would be on opposite sides?"

"Well, I *am* seeing you." He had the nerve to smile at her. "Who cares if we're in different groups?"

Lillie pointed at herself. "*I* care!"

Jay's back stiffened and he gave her a cool look. "I never realized before that a person can't be your friend unless both of you agree about everything."

"That's not true! I didn't say that," Lillie snapped.

"No?" Jay raised one dark eyebrow. "Then why are you so upset? I'm just standing up for my opinion, the same way you are."

Lillie took two deep breaths. She was trying to control her emotions, but her voice grew louder as her temper heated. "I can't believe you, Jay Carson! You stood in my living room and talked to my dad about the strike. What are you? Some kind of spy?"

"A *spy*?" Jay's voice increased a few decibel

levels too. "Just because I disagree with you? Education is a fundamental American right, and teachers should not be allowed to deprive their students of that right!"

Lillie scowled. "You think my dad *enjoys* being on strike? He loves teaching! But the strike is necessary. *He* has a right to a decent salary, and if he can't get it any other way, he has a right to strike!"

"And *I* have a right to graduate!" Jay yelled.

"You'll graduate with the rest of the senior class," she told him angrily. "No one is going to deprive you of your precious diploma." She would never have guessed that Jay would get so excited about a piece of paper.

"And another thing—I'm supposed to start my summer job on June tenth. How can I do that if I still have to go to school?" he said.

"A job? You're this frazzled over a *job*? No wonder you're siding with the taxpayers!" She couldn't help speaking her thoughts out loud.

"It's not like I'll be dipping french fries in hot oil at Burger House," he said sarcastically. "If I *ever* get out of this high school, I'll be an intern in the editorial department of the *Middleton Gazette*."

Lillie was almost impressed. Very few high school students got summer jobs at the city newspaper—but she didn't want to think about that. "That's a cop-out, Carson! You want the strike settled for personal reasons. What about the teachers? What about *their* reasons?"

Out of the corner of her eye, Lillie saw the reporter and cameraman creeping closer and closer to them. She wondered how long they had been listening to the argument.

But Jay didn't seem to care that they had an audience. "The strike is wrong. The teachers are wrong. There is nothing right about what is going on!"

Lillie was so furious now that she could hardly speak. When she regained a little self-control, she retorted, "*You're* wrong, Jay. You're only thinking of yourself. Try thinking about other people for a change—like my dad . . . and me!" She turned to leave before he could reply.

But she didn't move fast enough to avoid hearing Jay's response. "I've been thinking a lot about you, Lillie. It's too bad I was wrong about you."

Anger surged through her as she strode purposefully back to her protest group. She didn't even bother to retrieve her sign. She just slipped back into her place between Gina and Karin.

"What happened? We could hear your voice way over here," Karin told her.

"Oooh!" Lillie couldn't find any words to describe her feelings. She had never felt so strongly about any boy. Just yesterday she had thought her feelings toward Jay were romantic, but now she was just plain mad. *Really* mad. And disappointed.

Jay Carson was the most infuriating person she had ever met. What had he meant by that last comment, anyway? Was she back on his mush-brain list? Not that she cared, she told herself.

When Frank started another chant, Lillie threw herself into the shouting with all her heart. Without a sign to wave, she thrust a clenched fist in the air as she yelled, "Free our school! Free our school!"

Chapter Nine

"Isn't it great that the sun's shining again today?" Karin said to Lillie at the park on Monday.

"It sure is, since we discovered the kids behave better outside than at my house." It sometimes seemed to Lillie that their little charges misbehaved on purpose so their sitters would take them to the park. "And am I ever glad that Tommy's grandmother wanted him to visit her in South Dakota!" Lillie added. "It's the only good thing that's happened in the past three days."

They found a shady spot under a tree. Karin spread out a blanket and Lillie began unpacking the supply bag. The children grabbed for the paper and washable paints. Without

Tommy to disrupt them, they went happily to work.

"That's a pretty picture," Karin told one of the boys. "I like dogs."

"It's a horse," he told her.

"Oh, sure. I knew it all the time," Karin said quickly.

"Hey, Evans!"

Lillie looked up to see who was calling her. It was one of the guys from the track team. She didn't know his name, but she'd seen him around school.

She gave him an uncertain wave and all the kids stared at him as he came over to her.

"Saw you on TV the other night. Thanks for telling Carson what to do with his attitude."

"You're welcome," she mumbled.

He was jogging off when another boy stopped by the blanket. "Hi, Lillie. You were great on the news Friday. Way to go!"

"Well, I—"

"Don't apologize for what you did," he told her. "I wish more of us had come to the protest. It looked like fun."

Lillie hadn't been planning to apologize. She just felt uncomfortable accepting compliments for arguing with Jay in front of a television camera.

104

"Lillie, are you famous?" Abby asked, wide-eyed.

Lillie twisted the chain that held her locket. "No."

"But I saw you on TV!" one of the kids announced. "You were yelling at some guy with long hair."

"It's only long in the back," Lillie said, embarrassed when she realized she was actually defending Jay. "And I didn't do anything special enough to be famous."

Karin threw an arm around Lillie's shoulder. "Hey, famous or not, you're still my best friend."

Lillie ducked her head before anyone could see the tears in her eyes. At that moment, it felt very good to have a best friend.

It was strange, the way she felt about Jay. When she thought about it, Lillie knew she wasn't still mad at him. The anger was gone, and it had left sadness in its place. Her heart felt very heavy. He might have been a very *special* friend, if only—

Karin snapped her fingers in front of Lillie's nose. "Wake up, Lillie, we need your help!"

"What?" She looked up quickly, expecting to see one of the children in trouble.

Instead, Karin held up two paintings that

105

two of the kids had drawn. "They want to know which one wins the award."

Lillie dug into the project bag and pulled out two yellow construction paper stars. After a moment's consideration, she pointed to the scribble drawing and said, "This earns the 'Best Use of Color' award."

Abby beamed with pleasure as Lillie taped a star to her shirt.

Her competitor looked very concerned until Lillie told him his horse deserved the award for the best animal picture of the day. His proud smile made her grin as she gave him his paper star.

When the children ran to the swings, Lillie said to Karin, "It's hard work, but sometimes it's worth it."

"Maybe." Karin didn't sound convinced. "*I* would have given him the award for the best *imitation* of an animal!"

Lillie laughed. "That's why I'm the official award giver."

She was glad their babysitting took so much of her time. Taking care of the children didn't leave her much time to think about Jay Carson.

"All right! We can be grown-ups!" Karin declared as she, Gina, and Lillie cruised into Middleton Mall late Wednesday afternoon.

"Grown-ups?" Gina stared at Karin's coveralls and her Snoopy earrings. "Try again, Donovan."

Karin shook her head. "Don't be so picky, Portelli. What I'm saying is, it's nice not to have a whole gang of little kids following us around. Right, Lillie?"

"Right." Lillie stuffed her hands in the pockets of her jeans and silently followed her friends through the mall.

Gina stopped in front of a window display. "Look at that swimsuit!"

"*What* suit?" Karin teased. "There's barely anything to it. And I bet it costs forty dollars."

"Should I try it on?" Gina looked at both of her friends, her dark eyes shining.

"Yeah, why not? Go ahead," Lillie told her.

"We'll come in and help you think of ways to convince your mother it's not indecent," Karin added.

While Gina disappeared into a dressing room with the suit, Karin and Lillie looked at some of the clothes in the store. Karin spotted the earring counter and walked over to examine the jewelry.

"Don't you just *love* these?" she asked Lillie, holding up an enormous pair of hoops.

"They're big enough for a dog to jump through." Lillie shook her head.

Karin wrinkled her nose. "You're not much fun today, Evans. Lighten up."

Lillie tried on a pair of sunglasses. For some reason, the idea of walking around in disguise appealed to her. She checked the price tag and quickly put the glasses back on the display card. No disguise was worth that much.

Gina came out of the dressing room with the swimsuit on the hanger and replaced it on the rack.

"Need a different size?" Karin asked.

"No, a different suit." Gina giggled. "I don't know what my mother would say, but *I* wouldn't dare wear it out of my house!"

Karin pulled the suit out from the rack, examined it, and nodded. "Good decision."

Lillie's stomach growled. "Are you guys hungry?"

"Starving," Karin declared. "Mandy stole my peanut butter sandwich at lunch."

"Let's go to Tacos Deluxe," Gina suggested. It wasn't the best place to eat in the mall, but they had been going there since they were in junior high school.

They raced down the two flights of stairs to Tacos Deluxe. Just as they picked up their orders at the counter, someone called, "Lillie Evans! I saw you on TV!"

People turned to stare. Lillie wished she had bought the dark glasses after all. She managed to smile at the two girls from her history class. "Hi, Paula. Hi, Vicky."

"Are you eating here?" Karin asked them. They nodded. "Why don't you sit with us, then?" Karin suggested.

After the girls finished their tacos, Karin had an idea. "Want to rent a movie and come over to my house?"

"Sure. We don't have any homework to do," Paula said, laughing.

Lillie didn't have anything better to do than watch a movie, either. But she didn't think it was funny. She was tired of babysitting with Karin every day and she missed all her other friends from school.

"So Jack believed it when Cecile told him Suzanne had been lying about the blackmail," Vicky said later on that afternoon.

"Wait . . . wait . . . !" Karin tried to get the story straight. "This is the worst thing about babysitting. We could be watching *Forever Together* every day. It's my favorite soap opera."

"Do you think it would make any more sense if we heard it again?" Lillie asked.

"No," Gina said, shaking her head. "I watch

it during lunch, but sometimes my brother makes so much noise that I can't hear the dialogue. Anyway, I *still* don't understand why Jack believed Cecile. Everybody knows she'd do anything to get Suzanne into trouble."

"I just hope that strike lasts long enough so we can find out if Jack breaks off the engagement," Paula said.

"That could take a month!" Karin cried. "I start my summer job the second week of June."

"I suppose I could tape it," Paula told her.

"My problem is sleeping so late," Vicky confessed. "I almost missed the show yesterday."

"But it comes on at noon," Lillie said. Maybe she could sleep that late just once before they all went back to school—if they ever did.

"Shh," Gina whispered. "It's time for the ghost!"

"What ghost?" Paula asked.

"In the movie," Karin said. "It's Gina's favorite part, but I hate it."

Lillie leaned against the wall and hugged one of the couch pillows to her chest. Why did the strike seem like an adventure to everyone else? She admitted it was a little exciting, but was she the only one who wanted things to get back to normal? She was supposed to have a history paper due next Monday, and her father had encouraged her to work on it, but the whole thing seemed so useless. Thinking about all the homework they'd probably have when the strike ended, she winced.

That was one of the many bad things about the strike. The teams were losing valuable practice time and forfeiting their games. They couldn't compete officially without a coach. And the seniors were worried about graduation.

Lillie refused to feel sorry for Jay. He wasn't the only senior. And he wasn't the only person who had a summer job waiting for him. Karin was worried that her job might be given to someone else if she was still in school, but that didn't mean Karin turned her back on her friends. She had marched with the teachers, supporting their right to fair pay. But then, Karin was a *real* friend.

Suddenly, Vicky and Paula were at the door, calling, "Bye, Lillie. Bye, Karin."

She had to rub her eyes before she could focus. Had she really fallen asleep on Karin's floor? She waved. "Sorry—guess I dozed off."

"No problem. This strike thing is totally exhausting!" Vicky joked.

After the girls were gone, Lillie yawned. "Maybe I should go home and get some real sleep."

Gina said, "No way. You're not going to leave yet."

"I'm not?" Had Gina and Karin made some plans that she had forgotten? Or maybe they had decided something while she was asleep.

"We think you need to talk." Both her friends sat down on the floor on either side of Lillie.

"About what?"

"Whatever is bothering you," Gina said. "You were so quiet tonight. You weren't yourself."

Lillie wondered who they thought she was being if she wasn't being herself. But her friends were serious.

Karin sighed. "It wasn't just tonight. You've been acting weird ever since . . . I guess since the demonstration."

"You know I'm upset about the strike," she told them. "It might be crazy, but I really want to go back to school."

"Are you sure it isn't Jay?" Gina asked.

Lillie's breath caught in her throat. "What about Jay?"

"We know he hurt your feelings last Friday," Karin said softly. "And I know you didn't like your argument having on the six o'clock news."

"But you won't ever have to see him again," Gina told her.

112

"I know." Lillie sighed. Which was worse? Seeing him or *not* seeing him?

She wasn't about to tell Karin and Gina how much she had started to like Jay. After he had betrayed them all at the demonstration, she refused to admit anything about the hopes and dreams she once had about him.

"Cheer up," Karin advised. "The strike can't last forever."

Gina added, "Just think—any day now they might settle their differences and we'll be back in school. We'll have too much homework to hang out at the mall or watch movies on a week night."

"I hope so," Lillie said, and both her friends moaned. Maybe things would be better when she got back into her old routines—routines from the days before she'd met Jay Carson.

Chapter Ten

"Look, the school's still there!"

"I was hoping maybe it had self-destructed."

"Why couldn't the strike last longer?"

"It was great! I listened to 'Passion Fever' for two whole weeks!"

Karin, Gina, and Lillie all turned to look at the last speaker. When they saw his zombie eyes and unsteady walk, they nodded in agreement.

Karin giggled. "Yeah. I bet he *did* listen to those heavy metal tapes—"

"Twenty-four hours a day for fourteen days," Gina finished.

Lillie had nothing to add. In fact, she didn't have much to say about anything as they went up the sidewalk to Newton High School.

"I was really surprised when the teachers

and school board settled their argument yesterday afternoon," Karin said. "Didn't you know about it, Lillie?"

"Not until my dad called home around four o'clock."

She had been happy about the news. In fact, less than an hour ago, she had been anxious to get back to school and put the strike behind her. Why was she so nervous now?

"I just wish we'd had a little more notice." Gina held out her right hand and waved a finger with a cracked nail. "I wanted to get this fixed before I came back to class."

Karin sighed as they pushed open the front doors and walked into the lobby. "It hasn't changed a bit."

When Gina had to duck to avoid a tennis ball being tossed between two freshman boys, she giggled and said, "I feel like we never left."

Lillie couldn't agree with her friends. She had expected a peaceful, welcome feeling to flood through her when she walked into Newton. Instead, she was so tense it was getting hard to breathe, and she knew what was wrong. It had a name: Jay Carson.

Before the strike, when she had walked

into school, she'd been looking for him around the front doors or hoping to see him at her locker. But now . . . Karin and Gina were wrong about things not changing while they were gone. Jay was not going to be part of her life. If she could be sure of one thing, it was that Jay would avoid her like the plague.

"Earth to Evans." Karin waved her hand in front of Lillie's face. "Do you read me?"

"Sure."

"You don't sound very convincing," Gina told her. "What's wrong?"

Rather than start a depressing discussion, Lillie said, "I guess it's just culture shock. I keep expecting Tommy Porter to jump out of my locker at me!"

Karin's hand flew to her heart. "That would be a daytime nightmare! Hush your mouth!"

"Don't tell her that," Gina protested. "Lillie has barely said two sentences all morning."

When her friends followed her to her locker, Lillie realized they weren't going to leave her alone. "Don't you have someplace else to go?"

Gina shook her head. "I have chorus first hour. I don't need any books."

"And I already have mine with me." Karin held out the books she had taken home on their last day of school.

Lillie peered into her locker. It smelled musty, another reminder that things weren't as they should be.

"Going to have lunch with us?" Gina asked.

"Yeah . . ."

Karin tapped her on the shoulder. "We'll be expecting you."

Lillie stared at her friends. Did they think she was so upset that she planned to starve herself? "I'll be there. And I promise to eat my fruits and veggies, okay?"

Karin stepped back in surprise. "What are you so touchy about?"

"I bet I know." Gina giggled. "She's got Ms. Russell first hour."

"Not Happy Camper Russell!" Karin covered her ears as if she couldn't stand to hear any more. "If you don't smile in her class, she sends you down to the office."

"Lillie's just using up all her grumpy looks before Ms. Russell sees her," Gina concluded.

"Not exactly," Lillie mumbled. Now her two best friends were making fun of her! She hoped her day would improve. Seven more hours of dumb jokes would be sheer torture.

"There she is—our favorite television star!" Bob called out as Lillie reached the student council lunch table.

"Knock it off!" Karin told him. "She's heard enough about that news broadcast."

Lillie sat down and scraped the extra mayonnaise off her fish sandwich. She had no interest in discussing the demonstration or the television broadcast.

"But I've got a question," Bob insisted. "Lillie, I didn't understand the last thing Jay said. It was something about how he'd been thinking about you and how he'd been wrong—"

"I didn't hear anything like that on the news," Frank said.

Karin whispered to her, "I bet he's making that up!"

Refusing to respond to Bob's comment, Lillie concentrated on separating the green grapes from the watermelon and cantaloupe in her fruit cup. She didn't want to talk about Jay Carson.

"Maybe it wasn't on the news." Bob paused before admitting, "I was waiting in the drink line. I guess maybe I overheard him say that."

"You were eavesdropping!" Gina accused.

"Can I help it if he was standing two feet away from me?" he asked. Then he turned to Lillie. "What did he mean? Were you dating him or something?"

Lillie didn't say a word.

Frank noticed her discomfort. "Smooth move, Wilson. Give her a break."

Both Karin and Gina waited until other conversations had started around the table before they leaned toward Lillie from both sides. Gina asked, "What's the deal?"

"I thought all you did was roller skate with him," Karin said, dying for more information.

"Was there more?" Gina asked.

"I kind of liked him, okay?" Lillie mumbled.

"And Jay? Did he kind of like *you*?" Karin wanted to know.

"That's a good question," Lillie said with a sigh. She had *thought* he liked her. But it wouldn't be the first time in her life that she'd been wrong.

Bob cleared his throat and used his student council voice to get everyone's attention. "Have you heard about the dance?"

"Who hasn't?" Frank said.

All morning Lillie had listened to teachers giving homework assignments. "What dance?"

The girl next to Frank explained, "There's a rumor that the administration is going to hold a Welcome Back Dance a week from Saturday."

"It's more than a rumor," Bob told them, sitting tall. "It's their way of getting things back on track around here."

"What a good idea!" Karin cried. "It's just what we need to put the strike behind us."

Lillie looked from one person to the next and found them all grinning at the idea. But she didn't think a dance was going to help to put the last few weeks out of her mind.

"I think we—I mean the student council—should do something to get everyone involved with the dance," Bob said. "What do you think about asking all the clubs to sponsor booths?"

"Great!"

"What kind of booths?"

"T-shirt painting, doughnut sales . . ." Bob listed the projects that had been used and reused since Lillie had been at Newton. He ended with, "I think the student council should sponsor a raffle. . . ."

Karin nudged Lillie. "He's looking at you. I think he just volunteered you to collect raffle prizes."

"What do you think, Lillie? Could you help us get some great raffle gifts?" Bob said. "You did a terrific job on the jump-a-thon."

"No." Lillie shook her head. "I can't ask the local merchants for more things so soon."

Everyone around the table fell silent. Lillie realized what she had just done; she had disagreed with Bob. And nobody argued with the student council president.

She waited for someone to speak. There had to be some other person who thought it was hopeless to expect a dance and a raffle to wash away the disappointments. In the back of her head, a small voice—Jay's voice—agreed with her. It said how mush-brained it was to think that a social event could resolve any real problems.

"I can talk to the drama people," one girl said.

"I'll ask the cheerleaders," Gina offered.

"How about a kissing booth?" Frank joked.

Lillie realized no one else at the table shared her doubts. They all seemed to think alike. Had they always been that way? Or had Jay Carson warped her mind and made her see them as he did? Jay had been full of interesting ideas. But Jay was gone from her life, and Lillie's other friends were still with her. She owed them something.

"Would you at least call the people who print our raffle tickets?" Bob was asking her.

"No problem." Lillie realized that a lot of people were staring at her. She had no idea what she had missed while she had been thinking about Jay. To be safe, she changed the subject. "Does anyone else have enough homework to last for a month?"

"Is that all that's wrong with you?" Frank asked, sighing with relief. "I thought you might have a real problem."

Lillie rolled her eyes. "To me, a math test on Friday is a major disaster!"

"What about my English paper?" Frank asked.

"You'll ace it. You always do," Bob told him.

Karin counted off her assignments on her fingers. "I've got history, math, English—and I haven't even been to my afternoon classes yet!"

"Need any help?" Frank asked.

"Yeah. Like a truck to carry all my books home," Karin told him with a laugh.

Lillie waited until the guys were gone before she took Karin aside. "I think Frank really wanted to know if you would study with him. I think he's interested in you."

Karin's mouth fell open. "Really?"

Gina punched her in the arm. "Didn't you see him staring at you?"

Karin gazed out of the lunchroom door. The boys were nowhere in sight. "What do I do now?"

Lillie forgot her own problems as she and Gina exchanged glances. They both knew that Karin didn't have any excuse for acting so silly—she had dated other guys before.

"Is there something we don't know?" Gina asked.

"Frank's so cute. . . ." Karin's voice was soft and wispy.

"How long has this been going on? Are your friends always the last to know?" Lillie teased, conveniently forgetting that she hadn't full confided in them when it came to Jay.

"Quit making fun of me, guys!" Karin said. "So I really messed up. What can I do now?"

"Meet him at his locker after school," Gina suggested.

"What if he isn't there?"

Lillie put a hand on Karin's shoulder. "Then he'll probably be waiting for you at *your* locker."

"You think so?" Karin's smile was so dreamy that Lillie almost laughed.

But this new romance was great, she decided. In fact, it might be just what she needed. If Frank was turning Karin's brain to Jell-O, her friend was going to need a lot of attention. And the more time she spent with Karin, the less time she would have to feel sorry for herself.

For the first time that day, Lillie felt as though things were under control. Between all that homework and frantic phone calls from Karin, she'd be too busy to worry about Jay.

Chapter Eleven

Lillie fanned herself with her hall pass as she waited in the school office for Vice Principal McFadden.

She had just sat down on the bench in the outer office when she saw him. He smiled and headed directly toward her. Lillie hopped to her feet.

"Good afternoon, Lillie," Mr. McFadden said. "How has your day been? Does it feel good to be back?"

"It's been nice seeing everyone again," she told him.

"No problems?" he asked.

Lillie reminded herself that she had talked with the vice principal a hundred times on student council business, so she tried to relax. "I have enough homework for ten people!" she said, smiling.

He nodded. "That seems to be fairly common today. Do you have time to talk about a solution?"

A solution to the homework attack? Of course she had time!

Lillie started down the short hall that led to his office. Mr. McFadden caught up with her and opened the door for her.

The vice principal didn't sit behind his desk; he leaned against the front of it and Lillie decided not to sit down in one of his visitor chairs. She rested a hand on the back of one of them. "Did you mean you're going to stop all this homework?"

He chuckled. "Not quite."

Lillie waited for an explanation.

"I can't tell the teachers not to hand out assignments. The teachers are worried that the students will fall behind, and I'm concerned that the stress will only multiply the pressures around here."

"Pressures?" Lillie echoed.

"Oh, yes." Mr. McFadden grew very serious. "There are students who are angry about the strike. Some of them are very angry at the teachers, and others are mad at the school board. And then there are some students who

128

didn't want to come back here at all. It's a very touchy situation." He smiled at Lillie. "I'd like you to be part of the solution."

"Me?" In Lillie's opinion, she was one of the worst people to help. How was she going to tell the other kids to relax when she couldn't follow the advice herself?

"You've heard about the dance?"

Was that all he wanted? Had Bob asked Mr. McFadden to convince her to help with the student council booth? "I really don't think I can ask the local business people to donate more prizes," she told him.

"Prizes? For what?"

"For the student council raffle."

"*What* raffle?" He sounded more confused than Lillie had been at lunch.

"The student council decided to have a raffle to raise money, but I'm not sure what for."

Lillie realized that the vice principal didn't know anything about Bob's plans. "Bob Wilson thought that if there was a raffle, more kids would get involved in the dance—"

Mr. McFadden shook his head. "I should have known that Bob would want a part of the action. But not this time."

"No?"

"We want to put on a dance that will be fun

for everyone. How can you have any fun if you're working?" When Lillie shrugged her shoulders, he continued. "We want this to be a healing dance for the school, not a fundraiser."

Lillie liked his way of thinking. Bob loved to turn everything into a student council display—they not only had to participate in every event; they had to be in charge.

"Wait a minute." Lillie cocked her head. "Why am I here if there's not going to be a raffle?"

"We need a little help *before* the dance," he explained. "We need to get the word out about it, and we want to encourage *everyone* to attend."

"How?" Lillie asked.

"Since you and Jay did such a great job with the jump-a-thon— "

"You want me to work with *Jay Carson*?" Lillie hoped she'd misunderstood him.

"Yes."

"But . . ." What was she going to tell him?

Mr. McFadden nodded. "I missed the protest march, but I saw you both on the news."

"Then you know we can't work together!" Lillie said.

The vice principal continued. "A lot of people saw the news that Friday night. To many of them, you and Jay became symbols of the two opposite opinions in this school."

Lillie let his words ramble around in her brain for a few moments, trying to understand what he wanted from her.

"You're saying that some of the kids at Newton agree with me and some agree with Jay?" When he nodded, she continued, "And you think they'll forget their arguments if they see Jay and me working together?"

"That's part of it. I'm also counting on you and Jay to produce a great campaign to get students to come to the dance."

Lillie sighed. "It's a nice idea, Mr. McFadden. Too bad Jay won't be interested."

"But he is. He wants to meet with you after school."

Jay had agreed to work on the project? He wanted to meet her after school? Impossible!

"I don't think so," she told him.

"He left this office just fifteen minutes ago saying he'd wait for you in the art room after school today. He's willing to do publicity for the dance."

Stop it, she warned herself as she left Mr. McFadden's office. *Don't you dare start hoping Jay's doing it because he wants to see you again!*

* * *

Lillie peeked into the art room. There were several people in there. Some were still packing up from the last class. Others seemed to be working. But she didn't see Jay. Maybe he'd changed his mind.

"Over here, Lillie," he called from the back of the room.

She felt her cheeks getting hot as she walked past the long art tables, convinced that everyone was watching her and wondering what was going on with her and Jay.

"Have a seat," he invited when she reached his table.

Assuming they might be looking at sketches, Lillie pulled out the chair next to his. But she moved it a few inches away from him before she sat down. She didn't want to give him the idea that she had agreed to the project just so she could see him again.

Shifting in her chair, she told him, "I'm not very comfortable here."

"Don't worry. We won't be here long," Jay said.

Lillie was disappointed that he didn't offer to take her somewhere for a soda or something. Although she had warned herself not to get excited about seeing Jay again, part of her had hoped *he* might have been happy to see *her*. And now it seemed like he was only interested in business. She felt like a balloon that had just been popped.

"Something wrong?" he asked.

"No . . ."

Jay pushed his chair back and stretched out his legs. "Let's get something straight. I don't want to be here any more than you do. I bet McFadden got you to agree to help with the dance before he mentioned my name, right?"

Lillie nodded. The lump in her throat was making it hard for her to talk.

"Well, we've both given our word. So here we are."

"Here we are," she echoed in a low voice.

"And since we agreed, we'll have to work together. Can we try to put aside our personal differences and get this thing done as quickly as possible?"

"Of course." Lillie took a deep breath. She was not going to let Jay see how much he was hurting her.

"So what ideas do you have for the campaign?" he asked her.

"Posters," she answered promptly. Lillie had been too nervous about seeing Jay again to give any thought to the actual project.

He sighed. "We did that last time. What

133

about stuffing fliers between the cracks in locker doors?"

Lillie had visions of freshmen turning all the fliers into paper airplanes and sailing them down the halls. Instead, she suggested, "We could put announcements on the lunch trays in the cafeteria."

"People would only throw them away." Jay folded his arms over his chest. "Look, Lillie, I guess we're not going to agree on anything major. But how hard is it to admit that fliers are a good idea?"

"Fine. They're wonderful." Why had Mr. McFadden gotten her involved in this thing? Jay could obviously do the whole thing by himself. "But I still think we need some posters."

"Okay." He reached for a notebook and a pen. "What are these posters and fliers going to say?"

"Isn't that supposed to be your big talent?" she said too sweetly.

Jay narrowed his eyes and stared at her. It occurred to Lillie that she'd never been sarcastic with him until now. What was happening to her? First, she'd argued with Bob, and now she was being snippy with Jay. Well, it was all his fault, she told herself irritably.

"I thought you might have one or two thoughts," he said in a bored tone.

"I suppose I might," she said, trying to sound as if it didn't matter. "I'll try to come up with a few slogans tonight between my math assignment and the thirty pages of history I have to read."

"You shouldn't be complaining," he told her. "I thought you wanted the str—" He stopped himself.

Lillie stiffened. What had he almost said? Was he blaming *her* for the strike and the homework? "What do you mean?"

Jay closed his notebook with a loud snap. "I think we should talk again in the morning. Think you might have some ideas by then?"

Lillie refused to look at him as she said, "I told you I would."

"Good. I'll meet you here at seven o'clock."

"Fine."

Chapter Twelve

Lillie was waiting in the art room the next morning when Jay stumbled in, brushing his hair out of his eyes. For a second, she thought his expression softened when he saw her. But if there had been any warmth there, it vanished immediately.

He sank into the chair next to her and slapped his sketch pad on the table. Without saying anything, he flipped to a page filled with scribbles.

"This is my idea." His finger traced across the page as he explained, "I think our posters and *fliers* should have a 'let's-get-back-together' theme."

Lillie snorted.

He glared at her. "What's wrong with that? I think it's exactly what McFadden wants."

"It is. I guess I'd expected something more creative—and more honest—from you."

"Are you accusing me of lying?"

"Not exactly. It's just hypocritical." How could the two of them plan a *get-together* theme, Lillie wondered, when they were so far apart?

He shoved his sketch pad aside. "I suppose you have a better idea?"

Lillie smirked. "I did have an inspiration last night between math and history. I'd go for some humor. What about hyping the dance as a break from the tons of homework we all have?"

"That's stupid!"

Lillie was shocked. Jay had never spoken to her that way before. She reminded herself that he wasn't at his best before eight o'clock in the morning, but he had been quite charming on some other mornings. The Jay Carson she had known before would have made a joke about her idea if he really hated it. He would have been kinder. But maybe she was just getting to know the real Jay Carson.

"No defense?" he taunted when she didn't say anything. "But then, how could you defend such a mush-brain plan?"

"*Mush-brain?*" She hated that name more than she'd ever hated any nickname, including being called Lillie-Liver in third grade.

Jay peered at her as if his intense dark eyes could see right inside her head. "How did your brain go soft so fast? I thought I'd been making progress with you."

"*Progress?*" Lillie was so angry that she had to struggle to control herself. "There was nothing wrong with me when I met you!"

"I imagine *all* mush-brains think they're perfectly fine," he told her smugly.

"Stop it!" she cried, clenching her fists.

"Stop what? Stop talking about what happened at the demonstration?" he asked.

"We're *not* talking about that! We're supposed to be trying to discuss the dance, and we were until you started insulting me!"

"Who cares about the dumb dance?" Jay stood up and shoved his hands into his jeans pockets. Then he started to pace. "You tricked me, and I'm mad!"

Thinking that he was referring to McFadden and the dance promotion, Lillie said, "I didn't trick you into getting involved in this dance deal. You agreed to work on it before Mr. McFadden ever talked to me."

Jay spun around and the expression on his face made it clear that in his opinion, she was even more stupid than he'd imagined. "Don't play games, Lillie. I'm talking about the strike."

She pushed back her chair and stalked to the opposite side of the art room. If he wanted to discuss the strike, that was fine with her. She had a few things to say on the subject, too.

"How did I trick you?" she demanded.

"You let me think you understood about people standing up for their beliefs. And then you almost exploded when I didn't march in your neat little circle." He rubbed his temples. "I knew we'd be on opposite sides, but that didn't mean we had to be enemies."

"Talk about tricking people!" she cried. "From the things you'd said about wanting the strike to be over, I thought we'd be on the same side."

He laughed out loud, but it wasn't an amused sound. "Me? Encouraging the teachers to keep on depriving us of our education?"

Lillie shook her head. "How was I supposed to know you'd turn *establishment* and join the taxpayers who don't want to pay the teachers fairly?"

"That's not the real reason," he said grimly. "I know what really happened that day. You blew your stack because my opinion was different from yours and your friends'. From then on, I wasn't good enough for you."

Lillie slapped her hand against her forehead. "You're out of your mind! I wasn't mad at you because we had different ideas. You were just so *insensitive* about the whole thing. You didn't even try to understand my feelings or my father's position—"

"I'm not responsible for your father's problems," Jay muttered.

"You could have tried to understand," she insisted. "But you were too busy thinking about yourself and your summer job. When I first met you, I was really impressed by your caring attitude. What happened to it?"

"You!" he snapped. "Why should I care about you or your father when you don't care about me or my job or my future?"

"I *do* care!" Lillie shouted.

Suddenly she realized how silly they were both acting. They were yelling at each other just the way the little kids in her babysitting group used to. Not sure what to do next, she giggled.

"What's so funny?" he demanded.

"Us," she told him. "What are we arguing about? We're supposed to be working on the dance promotion. The strike is over."

"Not between you and me, it isn't!" he yelled and stormed out of the room.

Lillie stood alone, tears stinging her eyes. How had it all turned out so badly? While she'd been suffering because she thought Jay had betrayed her, he'd been blaming her for abandoning him and siding with her other friends. They had both made mistakes. Was it too late to fix them?

She noticed he had left his sketch pad on the art table. Knowing he would come back for it, she sat at the table and wrote him a note on one of the sheets of paper:

> Jay,
> Your idea for the dance posters and fliers is great. I'm willing to help if you still want me to. Let's talk.
>
> Lillie

It wasn't exactly true. She still thought her idea was pretty good, but this wasn't the time for fighting over details. She'd compromise on the dance campaign if it meant she and Jay could clear the air between them.

Lillie read her note once more. She had never written an apology to anybody. But it wasn't quite an apology; it was more like a plea for a second chance. Hoping it would work, she tucked it inside his sketch pad where he would be sure to find it.

The next step was up to him.

*　*　*

Lillie was a wreck by the end of the day. Between classes she'd been watching for Jay in the halls. She had barely been able to eat her lunch, hoping he would find her and have something to say. Her stomach was twisted into tight knots as she approached her locker. If he wasn't there, it meant that he didn't care about her at all.

"Hey, Evans."

"Oh, it's you," Lillie mumbled when she saw Karin leaning against her locker.

Her friend pouted and moved aside. "Who were you expecting? Prince Charming?"

Lillie spun her locker dial and sighed. "Something like that."

"A new guy?" When Lillie didn't answer, Karin guessed, "Not Jay again!"

"Maybe. Probably not." Lillie sighed again. "I don't know." If she was smart, she'd forget him. But it was impossible not to remember the way she'd felt when he looked at her and when he held her hand.

"Mind if I tell you my good news?" Karin asked.

"Good news?" Lillie examined the sappy expression on her friend's face. "Could this have something to do with Frank?"

Karin beamed and nodded.

"Well, what happened?" Lillie asked. "Are you going out with him?"

Karin nodded again. "Friday night, if I survive until then! I've got a chemistry test tomorrow. But I shouldn't be talking about myself. What can we do about *you*?"

"I'll be fine." Lillie needed a break from worrying about Jay. "Let's stop by the student council office. Maybe *someone* we know will be there. I bet Frank would be a great chemistry study partner."

"Good idea!" The girls ran up the central staircase two steps at a time, and as Lillie had suggested, they headed for the student council room.

"Hi, Karin." Frank smiled at Karin, then glanced at Lillie and pointed to the big envelope on the desk. "There's something for you."

She recognized Jay's handwriting immediately. Karin and Frank were busy talking, so she sat on the edge of the desk and studied the envelope, almost afraid to see what was inside. What did he have to tell her that he couldn't say in person?

Slowly, she slid a handful of thick sheets out of the envelope. They were sketches of the posters and fliers Jay planned to make. She smiled as she reviewed his ideas. There was a cartoon of a tuba player discussing the dance with a flute player. The next was a cheerleader and a football player. Gazing at

144

the last drawing, she realized he had included every group in the school.

Lillie opened the envelope wider, looking for another slip of paper, but there was no personal note. He had ignored her attempt to patch things up between them.

Frank and Karin were so wrapped up in each other that they didn't even notice when Lillie slipped into the hall. She decided to take the drawings back to the art room where Jay could find them in the morning.

What did you expect? she asked herself sadly in the empty hall. Jay Carson was obviously too busy with his cartoons and his political causes to be interested in a relationship with a girl like her.

The art room was empty. Lillie put the envelope containing the sketches on the table where her friendship with Jay had officially ended that morning. There was no reason for her to leave another note. There was nothing left for her to say.

Chapter Thirteen

"Are there any new posters today?" Gina asked Lillie.

"I have no idea," Lillie replied. The first posters and fliers had appeared on Tuesday morning. More were added on Wednesday. Lillie had no idea what Jay had planned for Thursday, but they would all find out soon enough.

Frank met Karin, Gina, and Lillie as they were walking down the hall. "You *have* to see this," he told them. He reached for Karin's hand and Lillie and Gina followed behind the couple to the band room.

"We've already seen the tuba player and the flutist," Gina said.

"That's what *you* think," Frank answered over his shoulder.

Lillie had heard that the music poster was an immediate hit with all the band members. Although she had seen the sketch, the finished drawing had turned out much better.

Frank and the girls weren't the only people who had come to the band room. There were lots of kids there, all talking about a *second* poster. Pulling Karin behind him, Frank pushed his way close to the wall where the poster was mounted. Lillie and Gina squeezed through the crowd after them.

"Oh, how cute," Karin gushed when she saw it.

Lillie stood on tiptoe to look over her friend's shoulder. In the cartoon, the flute player was holding her instrument over her head as if she were threatening the tuba player. She was asking him, "ARE YOU GOING TO OOM-PAH ALL WEEKEND? TAKE ME TO THE DANCE!"

Lillie loved the cartoon—it actually made her laugh out loud. It was so silly, unlike anything she would expect from Jay Carson. And she knew that Jay didn't believe that the dance was the answer to everyone's problems. She doubted he would even be there on Saturday night—not that she cared.

But listening to the kids talk and laugh about the new poster as well as the others scattered around the school, Lillie realized that the healing process had begun. His posters appealed to all the students, and he had given every group their own personal invitation —the musicians, the athletes, even the grad grinds. She hadn't seen one aimed at the student council yet—maybe he knew they would all be at the dance anyway.

"Hey, Gina," someone called. "Did you see the cheerleader poster by the trophy case?"

"Not yet," Gina called back. "Tell me about it, Alison."

"It's great," Alison said. "She's with a big football player who happens to look a lot like Johnny."

"Does the cheerleader look like me?" Gina asked.

"More like Diana," Alison had to admit. "But that's okay, because she's stomping on the guy's foot, saying, 'WHAT DO YOU MEAN, YOU'RE NOT TAKING ME TO THE DANCE?' "

Gina choked back her giggles. "Is Diana mad?"

"I don't think so. I think she's flattered that Jay put her in one of his drawings."

The kids around them mumbled in agreement. It seemed everyone would love to be in one of Jay's cartoons. Lillie was amazed. And to think she'd once been afraid he would do a nasty drawing of her!

Someone tapped her on the shoulder and said, "Good work, Lillie."

She turned to see Bob grinning at her. "What did I do?" she asked.

"I know Jay Carson didn't think up all this funny stuff on his own," he said.

"But he did," Lillie told him. "I didn't have anything to do with it."

"No?" Bob raised his eyebrows. "I didn't think Carson had that kind of sense of humor. Or did you change his attitude?"

The idea that she could have turned Jay Carson into a mush-brain made Lillie laugh. "I don't think *anyone* could do that!"

"Then how did he come up with these ideas?" Bob asked.

"Are you bugging Lillie about Jay Carson again?" Frank sounded disgusted.

"I'm just trying to get the whole story out of her," Bob said. "We all know McFadden asked her to help with the dance promotion, and Jay did the drawings. It's not hard to add two and two and get four."

"In this case, you get five," Lillie told him. "Mr. McFadden wanted us to work together. I guess he thought it would help if Jay and I could settle our differences, since our fight had been so public."

"See?" Bob grinned.

"But that's only part of it," she said before Bob could get any more pleased with himself. "Jay and I tried to work together, but we failed miserably, so he's doing this project on his own. While I've been home studying every night, Jay has been making the posters. I don't know any more about it than the rest of you."

When Lillie turned to leave, she found that the crowd had grown. She supposed they all wanted to hear the latest gossip, and she hoped they had heard enough, because she didn't plan to discuss it again, ever.

After lunch, Lillie was on her way to her first afternoon class and thinking about her English assignment when she saw Jay coming toward her down the crowded hall. He looked cheerful. Apparently he wasn't feeling awful about how things had turned out, the way she was.

His long hair was pushed back, revealing his ear stud, and his dark eyes were shining. Lillie guessed he was probably working out some new project in his head.

On impulse, she called out, "Great job on the posters, Jay."

He stopped right in the center of the busy

hallway. Lillie saw people bumping into each other to get around him, but she didn't want to wait for his reaction and risk a public rejection, so she kept on walking. She knew it was foolish to hope he would smile and thank her for the compliment. It was more likely that he would sneer at her and say loudly, *What's that supposed to mean, mush-brain?* All the same, she couldn't help feeling disappointed.

Gina and Karin caught up with her a moment later. "What happened to you?" Gina asked.

Karin added, "Did you fail a test? You look awfully blue."

"I saw . . . him," Lillie murmured.

Gina groaned. "Him? You mean Jay?"

"He's the one," she admitted, staring at the floor.

"What happened? Did you talk?" Karin asked.

"Don't be such a dope!" Lillie snapped.

Gina shook her head and turned to Karin. "I guess that means they didn't talk."

"Maybe you can get something going with him at the dance on Saturday," Karin said.

"Jay? At the dance? No way," Lillie said.

Karin pointed to a poster across the hall.

"But he did all this work. Of course he'll show up."

"No, he won't." Lillie knew enough about Jay to know he would rather get a tooth pulled than hang around a high school dance. "And I won't be there, either."

"What?" Karin could not have sounded more surprised if Lillie had declared she was dropping out of school and moving to the South Pole.

"Not go to the Welcome Back Dance?" Gina sounded indignant.

Although her friends were making it seem like she was neglecting her patriotic duty, Lillie refused to change her stand. It had been a sudden decision, but she knew in her heart that it was the right one. If Jay *was* there, she'd be miserable knowing he was avoiding her. And what would she do if he brought another girl? Lillie still believed he would skip the whole thing, but that wouldn't make it any easier for her. She could just see herself spending the whole night wishing things had worked out between them, and she could do that perfectly well at home.

"You have time to change your mind," Karin told her.

Gina smiled. "Karin's right. I don't care

what you say today—we'll see you at the dance."

Lillie lagged behind them on the way to class, determined to let them think whatever they wanted. But seeing Jay had proved to her that she hadn't gotten over him yet. Until she could pass him in the hallway without suffering a nervous attack, she was not going to risk being hurt by him again.

Chapter Fourteen

"What's going on?" Lillie asked as she, Karin, and Gina approached their lockers on Friday morning before classes began. There was a crowd of kids standing there, talking and looking at something. Maybe she was dreaming, Lillie thought. After she had finished her English report near midnight, she had tossed and turned until morning, and she was still half asleep.

But when she looked again, the crowd hadn't disappeared. In fact, it had grown larger.

"Maybe the security guards are raiding somebody's locker," Gina guessed.

"Don't be so negative," Karin argued. "I bet someone has a birthday and their friends did some decorating."

Lillie walked faster. "Let's see who it is."

The kids stepped away as the three girls came over, and Lillie realized that they were all watching her. More than anything in the world, she wanted to run out of the front doors and never come back to school. She was still glancing from one student to another for a clue when her friends started to giggle.

Then Karin moved aside and Lillie caught sight of her own locker. A poster was taped to her locker door—the artwork and style were unmistakable. She had wondered why Jay hadn't done a poster for the student council, but now she knew he'd been saving it just for her.

The drawing showed a girl with flowing hair. Her big eyes were angry, and her eyelashes were so long they cast shadows over her cheeks. And just in case Lillie didn't recognize herself, he had drawn a heart-shaped locket around her neck. The girl was holding on to the chain with one hand the way Lillie always did when she was nervous.

Lillie glanced down and noticed she was clutching the locket without realizing it. She yanked her hand away as if she'd been burned.

Suddenly Karin cried, "Lillie! You have to see the other one!"

"There's more?" She wasn't sure anything worse could happen. Following her friend's direction, Lillie turned.

She couldn't help smiling when she saw the poster on the locker directly across from hers. The cartoon was of Jay. Apparently he saw himself as tall and skinny with spindly legs and huge feet. His hair was wavy and out of control. The dark eyes were narrowed; his brows were drawn together in a scowl. The figure was leaning against a locker pointing his finger. His target was clear—the Lillie cartoon across the hall.

She was so fascinated with Jay's caricature of himself that she almost missed the bold words printed in a bubble over his head. When she read them, her mouth fell open.

DANCE WITH ME. FOR ONCE, DON'T ARGUE. JUST SHOW UP.

"He wants her to meet him at the dance!" Gina cried.

Lillie was speechless.

"Are you going to be there?" Karin asked Lillie eagerly.

"Of course she is," someone called from the group of spectators.

"I don't know. . . ." Lillie mumbled.

"You *have* to meet him there," another girl called. "This is like a dare."

"You can't back down on a dare."

"That's right," Gina said. "You've got to go, Lillie."

The five-minute warning bell rang and the crowd began to disperse. Lillie stuck her tongue out at the cartoon of herself before she opened her locker.

"What a day!" Gina said with a sigh.

"And it's only just starting," Karin added.

Lillie groaned. It was going to be so hard to sit through her classes when all she wanted to do was think about Jay's extraordinary invitation—or command. What had possessed him to make a public spectacle of them both?

Something inside her urged Lillie to interpret the posters as an apology, Jay's own personal way of saying he wanted to give their relationship a second chance. Or maybe he had just wanted to embarrass her for the terrible things he seemed to think she had done to him. What on earth was she going to do?

"Where have you been?" Karin demanded several hours later when Lillie finally met her friends outside the cafeteria.

Frank had a twinkle in his eyes when he

told her, "Karin and I figured Jay had kidnapped you."

Lillie laughed. Frank had always been nice, but he was even more fun now that he and Karin were dating. She said, "I wasn't sure I'd ever get to eat lunch. I can't go anywhere without being stopped by somebody who wants to know if I'm going to meet Jay at the dance."

"Hey, Lillie. You going?" one of the track team members called as he passed.

"See what I mean? And I don't even *know* that guy. How does he know me?"

"Maybe he recognized you from the drawing," Gina joked.

"I bet that's it," Frank said with a grin. "But answer his question for us. *Are* you going to the dance?"

Lillie took a deep breath. She had finally made up her mind. "Yes," she said.

Karin gave her a hug. "Then I'm going to help you decide what to wear. *Everyone* will be watching you, so you'll have to look great!"

"Does this mean our date is off?" Frank asked with concern. "I mean, do you need to hang out with Lillie tonight to prepare for the dance?"

"Do you think I need *that* much help to look presentable tomorrow night?" Lillie teased.

Frank's face turned pink. "Oh gee, no! I think you always look good."

"Thanks." Lillie felt her own cheeks growing warm.

Karin had no time for small talk. Pulling Lillie along toward the food line, she said, "I think your blue jumpsuit is nice. But maybe your mom has something super at the store. Let's check it out after school. . . ."

"Thanks for the ride," Lillie told Frank and Karin the next night as they entered the brightly decorated gym. "If I'd had to come by myself, I probably wouldn't have come at all."

People seemed to sense Lillie's arrival. All around the gym heads turned toward the door, but Lillie pretended not to notice.

"You want us to stay with you for a while?" Karin asked.

Lillie would have loved to be with her friends, but Gina was with Johnny and Frank obviously wanted to be alone with Karin. "No, I'll be fine."

Karin studied Lillie's face. "Are you sure?"

Pointing to Frank's tapping foot, she told her friend, "Look at this guy—he's dying to dance. It would look pretty weird if the three of us danced together."

"If you're sure . . ." Karin was reluctant to leave her.

Frank slipped his arm around Karin's waist and told Lillie, "I'm going to take her away now. But if you need any moral support, we'll be here. And if you need a ride home, promise you'll ask."

"Thanks so much." Lillie automatically reached for her locket, but she had left it at home. It hadn't looked right with the outfit from her mother's store. Feeling nervous, she buried her hands in the pockets of her short leather skirt. Her mom and Karin had said it looked good with the peach-colored silk blouse. Personally, Lillie's favorite part of the outfit was the brown and peach tapestry vest.

Karin had loaned her a pair of dangly silver earrings, and they had spent an hour braiding her wet hair that morning to give her a head full of waves. She looked entirely different than she usually did. What if Jay didn't recognize her?

A sudden shiver zigzagged down her back. Without seeing or hearing him, she knew Jay was right behind her.

Slowly, she turned to face him. He looked the same as always. His jeans were old and worn, and his leather jacket was open over an IT'S YOUR OZONE LAYER TOO T-shirt. But there

161

was something new in his expression. He didn't look angry the way he had at the demonstration. Nor did he have his usual cocky, confident look. He seemed almost uncertain, as uncertain as Lillie felt.

She shifted nervously as he studied her. His gaze traveled from her wavy hair to her bare neck to her short skirt to her boots. One corner of his mouth lifted in a half smile. But what was he thinking?

"Did you do all this for me?" he asked.

The entire gym seemed to fall silent except for the music. Lillie almost expected the Channel Four reporter and cameraman to rush into the room, covering their meeting for the ten o'clock news.

When she didn't answer, Jay leaned closer to her and said, "Let's dance. We can talk later."

Their hands met. Trying to ignore all the curious eyes on them, they walked to the center of the gym as a slow, romantic song began to play.

Jay slid his arm around her back and they both started swaying to the music. Although she wanted to hide her face and close her eyes to block out all the interested onlookers, she didn't quite dare rest her head on his chest. Until they talked, she wasn't going to do anything that might prove embarrassing.

The next song was a fast one. And the next. And the next. Jay and Lillie kept on dancing, and Lillie was beginning to doubt whether they would ever get a chance to talk. Then she heard the opening chords of a Skye number.

"Oh, good." Lillie sighed with relief. Skye was her favorite singer. Her songs were about love and commitment—and they weren't fast.

"You like slow dancing?" Jay asked, smiling.

"I love Skye's music. And I need a break." She panted like a dog to make her point.

"Would you like something to drink?"

"That would be fine." Now that they weren't dancing, she felt awkward with him.

As they walked to the refreshment table, Jay said, "So you like Skye?"

"I think her songs are great," Lillie told him. When he hesitated, she asked, "You don't agree?"

"I think her songs are, well . . ." When he paused, Lillie cringed. She thought he was going to say the songs were mush-brained. Instead, he finished with, "sugary."

"What kind of music *do* you like?" she asked, genuinely interested.

"For listening . . . well, you heard my fa-

vorite radio station in my car. But for dancing, I like something loud and fast."

"And exhausting," Lillie added.

At the refreshment table, Jay groaned.
"They don't have any cream soda!"

"Cream soda?" Lillie gagged. "I *hate* that
stuff!"

"You're kidding. How can you . . ."

Lillie sighed in frustration. "It's hopeless.
We'll never agree—"

Before she could finish her sentence, Jay
leaned down and stopped her with a quick
kiss. Stunned, she felt her knees begin to
buckle. Jay grabbed her and whispered in
her ear, "We have to talk. Follow me."

Holding on to his hand, Lillie let him guide
her out of the gym, across the lobby, and
outside to the open courtyard. When her eyes
adjusted to the dimmer light, she noticed
several couples cuddled together on the benches.

Since there were no seats left, Jay led her
to a vacant spot along one wall. He just looked
at her for several minutes. Then he gently
brushed away a strand of hair that had blown
into her face. "Lillie, I've been thinking about
you a lot since our fight," he said.

"Since our last *big* fight?"

"Since I read your note."

He hadn't been the only one doing a lot of

thinking. Lillie had to know how he felt. Crossing her fingers for luck, she asked, "What did you decide?"

"Well, we obviously have intense feelings for each other. . . ."

"Intense? You mean we're always going to fight?"

"Sometimes we'll fight," he admitted. "But lately it seems like *all* our emotions have come out as anger. I mean, I have a lot of feelings about you, and when things didn't work out like I expected, it was easier to turn all those feelings into anger than to think about what I really wanted. Does that make any sense to you?"

The sincerity in his dark eyes touched Lillie's heart. "It makes sense. I think you're saying there's some kind of chemistry between us. But lately it's turned into bad chemistry."

He smiled. "Exactly."

"So now what do we do?" she asked.

"I think it might be very interesting to see what we could do with all this energy—or chemistry—if we didn't waste it arguing."

"But we'll still be the same people," she told him. "We're still going to disagree."

"A lot," he said with enthusiasm. He touched

her under the chin. "Talk to me, Lillie. Tell me how you really feel."

Lillie shivered as his hand moved to the back of her neck. When she tried to reply, she forgot the question. "What did you ask me?"

"I asked how you really feel about . . . things. Do you think it's necessary for two people to agree about everything?"

"Well . . ." She hesitated. "Sometimes it gets boring when everyone thinks the same way."

His eyes sparkled when he smiled. "It can be more fun *our* way."

"As long as you don't yell at me and storm out of the room," she told him.

"We'll take time to talk things over." Jay bent down to kiss her softly on the forehead. Then he said, "Our friendship fell apart because we were both so busy blaming each other that we never really discussed our differences."

His tone made Lillie feel brave. "So, Jay Carson, are you telling me we could be friends?"

"Just friends?" he teased.

Lillie gazed into his eyes. Then she put her arms around his neck and pulled him toward her. But once they were nose to nose, she wasn't sure what to do next. Although she'd been kissed before, she had never been the one to start it.

Jay grinned. She knew he wasn't going to help her out. Tipping her head to one side, she pressed her lips to his. He wrapped his arms around her and held her very close.

Lillie sighed when the kiss ended. She should have known kissing Jay would be different from kissing anyone else!

"I think we agreed on that topic," he told her, wrapping a strand of her hair around a finger. "But I'm not sure about this 'just friends' stuff."

"You're not?" Lillie murmured.

"Don't you think maybe we could be more than friends?" he asked.

Lillie smiled. This was better than anything she had dared hope for when she was wishing for a second chance.

Jay's breath tickled her ear as he whispered, "Lillie Evans, there's a definite possibility that I love you."

Lillie grinned. "Would it be too boring if I said I love you, too?"

He stared at her as if he couldn't believe what he'd just heard. "You feel the same way? That's unbelievable! If you're telling the truth, I don't care if you argue with everything else I say tonight."

"You mean we're going to fight some more?" Lillie asked demurely.

Jay hugged her close. "Let's argue tomorrow," he whispered as his lips softly brushed against hers.

All-Star Movie and TV Favorites
The Hottest Teen Heartthrobs!

These terrific star bios are packed with the juicy details *you* want to know. Here's the inside scoop on the star's family life, friends, tips on dating, life on the set, future career plans, *plus* fantastic photo inserts.

☐ ALYSSA MILANO: SHE'S THE BOSS by Grace Catalano   28158 $2.75
☐ RIVER PHOENIX: HERO AND HEARTTHROB by Grace Catalano   27728 $2.75
☐ KIRK CAMERON: DREAM GUY by Grace Catalano   27135 $2.75

From the World of Rock!

☐ DEBBIE GIBSON: ELECTRIC STAR by Randi Reisfeld   28379 $2.95
☐ NEW KIDS ON THE BLOCK by Grace Catalano   28587 $3.50

☆ Plus...don't miss exciting movie and TV tie-ins of these top favorites!

☐ DEAD POETS SOCIETY by N.H. Kleinbaum   28298 $2.95
☐ HEAD OF THE CLASS by Susan Beth Pfeffer   28190 $2.95

Buy them at your local bookstore or use this handy page for ordering:

Bantam Books, Dept. DA29, 414 East Golf Road, Des Plaines, IL 60016

Please send me the items I have checked above. I am enclosing $_____ (please add $2.00 to cover postage and handling). Send check or money order, no cash or C.O.D.s please.

Mr/Ms _____

Address _____

City/State _____ Zip _____

DA29–3/90

Please allow four to six weeks for delivery.
Prices and availability subject to change without notice.